Table of Contents

Page
5 .... Prologue
7 .... Chapter 1 – St. Bartholemew's church -1900
15 .... Chapter 2 – Jubilee Park 1949
23 .... Chapter 3 – One week later
37 .... Chapter 4 – The next day after school
43 .... Chapter 5 – The next morning
55 .... Chapter 6 – Evening the same night
65 .... Chapter 7 – Fairyland
70 .... Chapter 8 – Talk of Angels
75 .... Chapter 9 – Fairyland – the cave of mirrors
84 .... Chapter 10 – Mons 1914
91 .... Chapter 11 – The dressing station
96 .... Chapter 12 – The retreat from Mons
100 .... Chapter 13 – 1900 - In the witch's lair
106 .... Chapter 14 - Billy's revenge
120 .... Chapter 15 - One week later – a terrible error
130 .... Chapter 16 - The retreat fom Mons – the find
134 .... Chapter 17 – After school
147 .... Chapter 18 – Emily meets the fairyland
157 .... Chapter 19 – Bob Helen reminisces
172 .... Chapter 20 – Fairytown
188 .... Chapter 21 – The invasion of Fairyland
201 .... Chapter 22 – Daniel and Emily
211 ....Chapter 23 – The reunion
237 .... Chapter 24 – The journey homeward
246 .... Chapter 25 – Loose ends
252 .... Epilogue – The present day

The Green Fairee in the Horthorn Bush

by

Christopher Bates

For my mother Sheila Bates who loves fairy stories.

Prologue

The village of Beare-in-the-Green had started out as an area within a royal hunting forest, later it passed to the church. At the time of the dissolution of the monasteries, it was sold and became part of the estate of a marquis, near to where the in the late eighteenth and early nineteenth century pheasants were raised for the then present marquis and his friends to shoot every w5inter in hays – a hay being the name of the area used for the raising of pheasants. The Marquis of that time was very into bloodsports, and as well as shooting game birds he loved the thrill of riding to the hounds and chasing the fox. He had an excellent stable and was master of the local hunt; for this he wore finely tailored hunting pinks – which were strangely red, rather than pink as their name might suggest - and also a rather dashing top hat made of golden cloth. Sadly, the habit of hunting foxes led to the end of his line. One fine January day in 1802 his son, the heir to his title, and his only descendent disappeared on a hunt. No body was found and the heartbroken marquis died a few years later without issue. The title died with him, and the big house which had stood at the centre of the estate, and had been expensive to maintain, was unwanted by his relatives who had expensive houses of their own so it was left to wrack and ruin. Within a few decades it had become a derelict ruin and was eventually pulled down. The site was used as a quarry with the masonry blocks gradually taken away for various building projects.

The estate was broken up and sold. The small village which had existed on the estate by the hay for the estate workers prospered and grew when coal was discovered, and miners from all over the country made their home there in the middle of Staffordshire, Jones's from Wales, Richmond's from Yorkshire and the like. Before long Beare-in-the-Green had become a small town with rows of terraced houses. Beare-in-the-Green benefited from good communications being on the railway mainline, which meant that the coal was easy to transport and the town continued to grow. Within a generation an area of countryside had become a little island of industrial urbanisation. By 1900, less than a hundred years after the last marquis had died and had been interred in the family vault of the church in the crypt of St.Bartholew's church, there was virtually nothing about the locality that he would have recognised – even the church beneath which his remains lay had been demolished and rebuilt.... and yet some things do persist – and for longer than we would wish if only we knew of their existence.

Chapter 1 – St. Bartholomew's Church, 1900

The church - St. Bartholomew's, in the parish of Beare-in-the-Green, lay inside a brick built wall. The top of the wall, which was about waist high to a man, was triangular in section and topped with metal caps of matching profile which supported a set of railings each topped with an ornate fleur-de-lys. Access to the churchyard beyond the wall was through the wooden lych-gate, a sort of open ended shed with gates on the outside with benches on either side of the inside. It was built of solid oak, weathered and darkened with age, it's roof was thatch, from a distance it looked like a tiny thatched cottage. The lych gate actually pre-dated the modern church, but it had been very well made, the thatch was periodically stripped off and refurbished, but the wood work, black with age was original, held together with various carpenter's joints and wooden pegs, or dowels known as wood nails from a time when iron nails were an expensive luxury, and the wooden alternative was cheaper, and easier.

The older visitors to the church remembered that the benches in the lych gate were not originally for sitting on but for the storage of coffins and the bodies contained within them, awaiting burial when frost and cold made the digging of a grave nye on impossible. In the days before mortuaries a body would have been safe and out of the way. This practice stopped with the advent of sack men, also known as ressurectionists or body snatchers. With the high prices paid by anatomists for fresh cadavers the idea of leaving loved ones unattended overnight fell out of fashion. In those days if the ground was too hard the body was kept at home or in an outhouse, or later still a mortuary, until a grave could be dug. A new fashion for wrought iron cages around graves for those who were rich enough followed to protect the interred, and two of these were visible in the churchyard – their bars serving not only as a safeguard but also beautiful expressions of the skill of the blacksmith, with their twisted and turned rods and floral finials. For everyone else there was the option of spending a few nights trying to stay awake to guard the grave of a loved one until the body would have putrefied underground enough to be of no use to the disectionists.

Near the path from the lych-gate to the church door was the most recent burial in the churchyard. The earth was still piled up on top of it topped with flowers which were still fresh with a film of silvery morning dew. The grave's size gave it away as that of a child. A simple temporary wooden cross was planted at the head of the grave. A more permanent headstone, which had been paid for by public subscription, and mentioned her long dead parents too, would replace the wooden cross once the ground had settled. Even though very few of the public could remember the grave's occupant it did not seem right that should have been a pauper's burial - not after such a long wait.

The church itself was not an old one, built fifty years previously; stone, unlike it's encompassing wall, rather than the stone used in an earlier church who's structure had fallen beyond reasonable repair. It was large enough to hold a couple of hundred people if you crammed them in. At the West end, over the door was a tower with a clock which was topped by a steeple which in profile reminded everyone of a witch's hat. Inside it was simple but pleasant. The far end with the organ and choir stalls ended in a semicircular construction with a matching half circular domed roof. The left side of the church had been extended outwards a few years after it had been built to accommodate the increasing population which had flooded the area as the local coal mines had been sunk and had provided employment for the menfolk. The architecture of the local streets was also by and large dictated by the miners – long streets of back to backs, and terraced houses, the later ones with entryways; dark arches between the houses that led through to the back gardens. Like it's surrounding streets St Bartholomew's was definitely Victorian in style but with all the features you'd have found in a church built a couple of hundred years earlier, a tall echoing roof, stained glass windows, a brass lectern in the shape of an eagle which held a large Bible and a stone pulpit, exquisitely carved with fluted columns, and arched panels reached by a short flight of steps. These items, along with some monuments on the walls and other fittings such as the organ, had been transplanted from the old into the new building. One of the stained glass windows showed a representation of St. Bartholomew himself, who in real life had been unfortunate enough martyred by the gruesome method of being skinned alive. To this end he was represented with a flensing knife in one hand and his flensed skin hanging like a floppy wetsuit in the other. Curiously he was always depicted in rude health – always a mystery to little children who wondered why he wasn't shown skinless and red raw with blood everywhere.

The vicar looked at the church congregation from the pulpit. Normally on a Sunday it could be described as full. Families occupied the pews with fidgeting children hemmed in between two watchful parents on each end of their brood whenever possible. Not too fidgety though – that might lead to a thick ear. Heaven help the child who showed their parents up in church when they got home.

Today, a Wednesday, it wasn't full, it was packed. The front row was filled with the family. School children, wearing their Sunday best and their teachers in their black gowns, their mortar board caps held in their hands whilst inside church as a mark of respect, took up pews behind. The rest of the congregation was made up of a cross section of the local populace, the overwhelming colour of the clothing was black. People stood in the aisle and squeezed in tight bunches at the back of the church.

The vicar had done his weeping in private, it was his job to be strong for his flock, but it was hard not to break under the emotion of a service like this. Plenty of people were weeping in the church though, amongst them Billy Richmond, classmate of Emily, the child who this service was all about. Missing for over two months and now presumed dead, the little girl with the terrible squint and the funny manner that he, among others, had found such sport in teasing. He regretted that now, really regretted it. Someone had abducted her so the rumours went – Gypsies probably if you were an adult, although no Gypsies had been reported in the area at the time. Others felt she'd fallen into an old mine ventilation shaft, but an intensive search had failed to reveal any such shaft apart from the ones already known about and those had a brick surround about them and in most, but not all, cases an iron grill over them. Those that lacked a grill had been investigated but nothing was found. The children said that she'd gone to be with the fairies; Emily had loved the idea of fairies, and her few friends stated that she made stories up about seeing them. In truth not many believed she'd gone away to be with the fairies, but it was a comforting camouflage for the nine year-olds who were her guilt racked classmates and who had previously been her tormentors. They'd tormented her for her belief in fairies, for the stories that she told about having them in her garden, and for her terrible squint. Billy prayed earnestly, he would do anything, go through anything to see Emily back and safe. Guilt was really taking it's toll of him. He looked up at the large marble memorial on the whitewashed wall behind the font at the front of the church opposite the pulpit and for the umpteenth time in the last two months he re-read it:

Robert Neville

lost to this world

Jan^{ry} 18th 1802.

Aged 11 Years.

"Death like an overflowing stream,

Sweeps us away. Our life's a dream,

An empty tale: a Morning flow'r

Cut down and withered in an hour."

and for the umpteenth time he burst into tears again.

Over the uncontrolled sobbing of Emily's mother the vicar

concluded his service with one last appeal for anyone who knew anything to come forward to the authorities, the police or even himself. The slightest thing might be of use to find the girl and give her parents some small comfort.

An old man in his seventies now and close to retirement he was unsettled by this whole thing. Shortly after he had taken up his incumbency in the parish as a very young man some forty nine years previously he'd had to perform a similar service for a little girl. The similarities were enough to make his flesh stand in goose bumps and icicles form along his spine. Enid, the first little lass, had last been seen playing on a piece of heath land near her home, which thirty six years later in 1887, had become a public park to mark Her Majesty Queen Victoria's golden jubilee. This was not only the last place she had been seen, but the last place that Emily had been seen, and in the course of the search for Emily, also the same place that a skeleton had been found. The size of the remains and lack of other missing children in the area had lead to them being identified as Enid, He had performed Enid's burial in the churchyard a few days previously - her grave was the fresh one beside the path. The coincidence that bothered him most was that forty nine years earlier, at the same time that Enid had vanished a set of bones had been found on what was the heath which at first were thought to be Enid. They had turned out to be the bones of a little lad lost half a century before Enid vanished.

Billy wasn't the only one who had recently spent a lot of time looking at the white marble memorial on the wall behind the font and wondering.

Billy listened to the vicar's words about coming and speaking to him. As the service ended he watched him process down the aisle of the church with its red, black, white and cream tiles, in his graceful black frock-like cassock, white slightly billowy surplice - which Billy thought on a windy night might have given him the appearance of a ghost - and black stole, with silver embroidered crosses at the ends, hanging down his front like an over long scarf from his shoulders, to stand just outside the door shaking hands and speaking to the people as they left.

Billy plucked up courage and decided to confide in him about something he had seen in the park a few days before Emily had vanished, some thing that might explain her disappearance, something that he hadn't told an adult because he would be called a liar, something that he hadn't told his pals because he feared the mockery that he had used on Emily being used on him. As he shuffled down the aisle he looked up at the vicar's face, he opened his mouth to speak and a strangulated sob came out. The vicar smiled sadly and patted him kindly on the shoulder, leaned down and whispered "God be with you Billy, have courage young man." Billy's nerve failed him and he walked past and decided that he must have imagined what he saw and made his mind up not to speak of it again.

Chapter 2 - Jubilee Park – 1949

The path hadn't been there before – ever. Daniel was sure of that; and yet there it was in the corner of the park where the gnarled old hawthorn bushes formed an impenetrable barrier between and around the trunks of two trees; a broad girthed oak with its grey scaly bark with it's ridges and crevases, and dense foliage, and a soaring ash with its longer finger like leaves. The lower branches of the trees intertwined with each other and rose out of the hawthorn mass, the joints to their parent trees hidden in the thorns. And there, in the middle was a path. It lead through the hawthorn which appeared to form a tunnel. It was cobbled with stones the size of a man's fist and was about two feet across. Thick moss grew between the stones, which shone faintly as if they reflected moonlight, but the stones themselves were free of moss. The sides of the hawthorn tunnel appeared to have been trained so that they intermeshed densely to form a tube about four feet in diameter into which not a single twig intruded, the tube followed the slightly weaving journey of the path exactly. It was dim and green in there. Daniel could see about twenty yards into the tunnel before it curved gently round to the right, not that Daniel could gauge twenty yards by eye - as a rule eight year old boys can't - but he knew the park railings were just behind the trees and that meant that the tunnel should be out across the pavement and into the road, and yet it didn't seem to be.

He stared for some minutes trying to work it out. The tunnel was impassive and stared back at him. Finally he turned his head round and looked across the park to see if anyone was close enough to see what was here. No one was. There were kids up at the other end of the park playing on the slide, the swings and the witches hat, which creaked and groaned in the distance as it swung eccentrically atop its pillar, with kids sat facing inwards around it's rim. His left foot abruptly moved a pace forward of it's own volition, he snapped his head back round violently and stared wide eyed into the tunnel. Had something changed or moved in there? Suddenly instead of being something puzzling it had become threatening somehow. And then something did move at the far end of the tunnel, it moved very fast, blurringly fast, with a slight but definite whirring sound. Something had been standing at the far end of the tunnel, blending in and it had shot back around the corner. Anything that could hide that well and move away that fast was outside of Daniel's experience, his body sucked in a huge breath of air in preparation as the fight or flight - (definitely flight!) - response kicked in. And then with horror he realised that what ever had been there still was there. Two golden eyes blinked and gave away the position of a face as it peeped around the bend of the tunnel at him. Daniel fled. Little legs pumped like the pistons on the mighty Railway expresses that thundered along the track which ran not far from his house. They carried him swiftly across the grassy parkland toward safety. He was sure that he heard that whirring noise again, like a bird's wings, and then worse, he thought he heard his name called softly behind him "Daniel...", he ran faster than he had ever thought possible. Don't look back! Don't look back! Every kid who has ever been chased by an unseen monster, or monsters, through the darkness or thick fog or smog knows that rule. As long as you don't look back it might not get you, if you look back and see it, then it will become enraged and catch you for sure. This was different though It wasn't dark or foggy or smoggy, and he had already seen it, so it must catch him mustn't it? The terror was absolute and he ran faster than he ever had done before, his lungs were bursting and burning like hot coals on a kitchen range. As he approached the park gates he felt himself slowing, and knowing he had nothing to lose, chanced a look back over his shoulder at the far corner to see what it was that would devour, or snatch him away. There appeared to be no sign of a tunnel. He stopped running and turned to get a proper look, gasping and panting as he did so. Everything was as it should be, no tunnel and more importantly nothing chasing him. Still, better to be safe than sorry, he carried on his running taking the shortest route home, the way across the pedestrian crossing over the railway tracks that would earn him the biggest hiding of his life from his mom if she ever found out. He hurled himself into the far end of the kissing gate that led across the rails and threw back the hinged gate to exit on the other side. A scream, deafeningly loud, shrill and sudden stopped him dead and he shot backwards into the gate as a huge green Castle class locomotive roared past yards in front of him at many miles an hour in a cloud of steam and smoke. Huge steel rimmed wheels glinted and spun past and there was the blurring motion of pistons, fleeting and then gone to be replaced by a stream of cream and chocolate coaches which flashed past him in a torrent of noise. Daniel was engulfed by a wonderfully rich smelling cloud of steam and smoke. The fireman, who had seen him a fraction of a second before he would have dashed to his death under the wheels and had blown the whistle to warn him, released the wire that operated it and leaned out of the cab shaking his grimy fist as the train sped away. His yelling and shouting was inaudible over the rushing, whooshing, rattling and roaring from the locomotive. As soon as he considered the guard's van at the back of the train to be far enough up the track as to be safe he dashed again across the track, realising half way across that he'd not checked in the other direction, he screeched to a halt, almost falling, checked both ways, and seeing nothing to indicate another train he took off again. Seven minutes later he was home, the entry way between the terraced houses stopped him short. It's dark brick interior and domed roof reminded him of the tunnel in the park. Still, he'd been through it almost every day of his life and the wooden door at the far end was open meaning he could see daylight at the end of it so he shot through, nothing grabbed at him, nothing whirred and he saw nothing that might have been looking at him with golden eyes. Quickly he locked himself in the outside toilet that lay in the yard beyond. He didn't need the toilet, but it was safe, and quiet in there and he could think. Nothing could get in there because of the bolt on the door. Whitewashed inside, it was quite bright with the light coming through the patterned window in the side wall, beneath which was the nail which held the loop of string with the squares of newspaper. Once seated he looked up at the black cast iron water cistern above his head mounted on its two brackets. He batted at the long, heavy rubber weight on the end of the chain which hung down from the left hand side of it. Something moved! Just a spider disturbed by the swinging chain. He grabbed the handle again and considered trying to squash the spider against the wall by throwing it. Was killing spiders bad luck? He couldn't remember. To be on the safe side he let the creature live – he didn't need any bad luck at the moment. Bad luck might mean the 'thingy' finding him. He slowly relaxed and tried to remember what he'd seen. The face that the eyes he'd seen had belonged to had been too far away and indistinct for him to recall it in detail but he thought it had been smiling. Not a nice smile, more like the sort of smile Johnny Steptoe the school bully used when he was intimidating smaller kids. Johnny Steptoe was not the biggest kid in the form at school - there were three who were bigger, all three were the ubiquitous 'gentle giants', indeed two of them were so gentle they were on occasion victims of the smaller Steptoe. He'd tried to make a victim of the third one too, but that had ended badly for Johnny when he found himself sitting on the pavement bleeding from the mouth and looking at two teeth on the floor. Gentle giants aren't always that gentle when they are roused and Johnny Steptoe's faith in the old wives' tale that 'The bigger they are - the harder they fall.' had been shattered; so much so that he moved onto easier, softer, and particularly, smaller targets.

Footsteps outside in the yard. Fast and urgent!
Realising that he'd been there some time piecing his thoughts together he stood up and out of force of habit he pulled the chain to flush the toilet, water rushed noisily down the pipe from the cistern to the porcelain toilet bowl. There was a sudden violent hammering on the door; he froze for a second.
"Daniel! Daniel are you in there? Come out at once!", The fact that it was his mom and not the whatever-it-was from the park was good news; the level of fury in her voice most definitely wasn't.
"Daniel, open this door at once or I'll belt the living daylights out of you!" she yelled. He wasn't stupid enough to fall for that one; she was probably going to belt the living daylights out of him whether he opened the door or not, but he reasoned that since he wasn't strong enough to hold the door if she tried to force it and the longer he left it the worse it was likely to be once she got in.

Also, if she got in he'd have nowhere to run, outside there was at least a small chance of fleeing.

'Please don't let her have found my fingerprint in the margarine ration!' he prayed as he cautiously slid the bolt back. He opened the door a crack; it burst open and a bony arm, bare to the elbow shot in. Daniel yelled as he was dragged by his ear blinking and squinting from the relative darkness of the toilet into the blinding rays of the setting sun. There was someone else there, oh heck, NO! Standing like a stony colossus behind his mom was PC Helen, he'd only heard his mom's feet, PC Helen moved quietly on rubber soled boots - all the better to catch you in the act!

Like most coppers of his generation he was a big man, six foot two in his stockings. An ex-infantryman, the row of medal ribbons on the chest of his tunic showed he'd served in Burma during the war. He was as hard as they came and he ruled his patch with a rod of iron. Kids in the street would quietly drift away as soon as they saw him and heaven help anyone stupid enough to give him lip when he deigned to speak to them, or anyone who forgot to deferentially call him Mr. Helen when they spoke to him, man or child. Johnny Steptoe said that it stood to reason that he was permanently angry when he had a girl's name like Helen. Johnny Steptoe also reckoned his dad had told him that Mr. Helen had a girl's Christian name too – Gertrude. That was really funny to a bunch of eight year-olds. Then one evening PC Helen had paid a visit to the Steptoes' and it was three days before Mr Steptoe had been able to go back to work at the coal mine, and when he did his face was still bruised. If you believed Mr Steptoe then the bruising was due to him being falling over drunk and that the PC's visit had been coincidental about a minor matter, the nature of which was vague and tended to vary a little depending on who Mr. Steptoe had spoken to. Johnny said someone had grassed his dad up for telling everyone Mr Helen's Christian name. Being eight year-olds everyone believed him. The adults on the other hand thought the bruises on Mr. Steptoe's face probably had something to do with the regular bruises which appeared on Mrs. Steptoe's face. Either way, her bruises never appeared again.

Daniel swallowed hard, his throbbing ear forgotten for the moment. He wondered frantically if telling Mr. Helen who it was that shot a stone through a bus window with their catapult earlier that week would make Mr. Helen go away. On balance probably not, and if it were ever found out that he was a copper's stool pigeon then the rest of his life at school would be hell. Best play dumb and deny everything.

"Where were you twenty minutes ago?" growled the officer.
"In the park Mr. Helen.", Daniel blurted out, his dumb act failing

at the first hurdle.

"And you came back across the pedestrian crossing instead of the footbridge half a mile down the road, nearly getting yourself killed by the express because you didn't look before you crossed!" shouted the officer.

"No Mr Helen!"

"You little liar!" - that was his mom, who was sniffing and wrinkling her nose like a deranged hedgehog, "You stink of smoke. How close was that train? You tell PC Helen the truth or I'll take the razor strop to your backside!"

Daniel opened his mouth and bawled,

"Wahhhhhhhhhh!", tears flooded down his little red cheeks from blue eyes which gave a very inappropriate impression of angelic innocence. Out of the corner of his eye, blurred by tears, he saw his mothers slap coming and ducked it but she was expecting it and got him on the back swing and now both his ears were throbbing. PC Helen stepped forward and grasped him by the front of his duffel coat lifting him onto his tip toes. Daniel continued to bawl like it was going out of fashion.

"Wahhhhhhhhhhhhhhh!"

"Listen you little idiot! If you had stepped in front of that train we'd have had to scrape you up with a trowel! The train would have had to stop, everyone on it would've been late home, and all the people on the trains following it! Your poor mother would've had to have found the money for a funeral and it would've meant a lot of extra work for me! Don't you ever go near that crossing again until you're old enough to have common sense! It's for adults not kids without brains. There's a footbridge half a mile up the road – use that! Do - you – under – stand!?" He shook Daniel at every syllable of the last question.

In between howls Daniel nodded like his life depended on it. PC Helen's grip slackened slightly, Daniel, saw his chance and took it, yanking free he was away like a greyhound from the slips, not waiting to see what would happen next. In through the kitchen door, and into the back room where his twelve year old sister Angela sat doing her home work at the table.

"Playing on the railway tracks were we? Naugh-ty – boy! I think I'll just go and fetch the razor strop for mom, I'm sure she'll be wanting it in a minute." She taunted, wagging her finger as he dodged across the room to the stairs in the corner.

"Shut up! I haaaate you!" he screamed as he flung open the door in the far corner of the room and pounded up the stairs behind it.

"I'd put a newspaper down the back of your shorts if I were you, 'cos you won't be sitting down for a while if you don't" he heard Angela's gleeful laughter following him as he went.

Angela sniggered to herself, put down her fountain pen, a Conway Stewart model with a gold nib and one of her most prized possessions, and picked up a well used piece of blotting paper to dry the ink on the page of her maths book. Daniel was going to take some stick for this little escapade over the next few weeks, she'd make sure of that. Not when mom was around though – that would be asking for trouble. Angela was good at avoiding trouble, but surprisingly good at causing it from time to time.

At the top of the stairs, and wondering what he had done to deserve a sister from hell, on top of PC Helen, passing locomotives nearly running him over and slicing him into bits, and the 'thingy' in the park, he reached the presumed safety of his bedroom. He slammed the door and feverishly dragged the white painted chest of drawer's across in front of it in the hope that if PC Helen or his mom took it into their heads to come up the stairs to give him a proper belting it would keep them out. That accomplished he sat down on the edge of his bed and started to grizzle properly. The afore mentioned razor strop, which had belonged to his late father, was kept by his mother as an ultimate sanction. A heavy, wide leather belt used for putting an edge on he blade of a razor it didn't see the light of day very often but when it did the marks lasted for quite a while as the did the throbbing pain. As he thought about it, and worried about it, the grizzling became longer and louder. Had there been prizes for endurance grizzling then Daniel would have had a shelf full of them, not to mention extra ones for style and presentation.

"He's not normally a bad boy Mr. Helen, but with his father dying in the war and everything." Daniel's mom pleaded.

"Doesn't make that much difference to the way a child behaves in my opinion Mrs. Smith." PC Helen replied, "Plenty of kids' fathers died in the war. Some behave, some don't, just like the lads who do have dads. I just hope I've put the fear of God into your son and he stays away in future. Daniel's not a bad lad, not like the little perisher I'm off too see now. I was on my way there when someone told me they'd seen Daniel on the tracks."

"Thank you ever so much Mr. Helen." and then because she couldn't resist fishing for a bit of gossip "Someone done something bad have they?"

"Yes. I've just found out that it was little Johnny Steptoe who put a stone through a bus window with his catapult earlier this week."

Chapter 3 - One week later.

It was the first time Daniel had been back to the park. He wasn't in the park yet, but he was stood round the corner from the gates in Hob Lane, across the road watching the hawthorn patch with the oak and ash sentinels. Their upper branches swayed in the stiff breeze that was blowing, occasionally there was a clack from branches slapping together as if the trees were sparring with each other. After five minutes, which is half a life time for an eight year old, nothing had happened.

If there had been a tunnel there then from where he stood the exit should have been visible, but there was nothing there. He crossed the road and stood a couple of feet from the railings, iron rods six feet high with points on the end. The corporation grey paint was bubbling off them where rust had forced it away and some of them were bent out of true. Daniel felt they formed a sufficient barrier to keep the 'thingy' away from him if it put in an appearance and maybe let him get a good look at it. A bit like the lions and stuff at the zoo; you felt safe at the zoo, dangerous animals which would gobble a small boy up as a snack were rendered harmless and powerless by a few iron bars. It seemed reasonable that the 'thingy' should also be contained safely where it couldn't get at him.

Still nothing happened.

Perhaps, like the lions at the zoo, the 'thingy' slept most of the time. The lions were therefore a bit disappointing, they only seemed to wake up if there was food in the offing. That thought brought him up cold, the very real possibility that he might be being regarded as food. Curiosity however gradually regained the upper hand. Through the railings he could see a stick. It was straightish, about the length of his arm and pale where all the bark had fallen off. Slowly he stepped forward, squatted and then never taking his eyes off the hawthorn patch he stealthily reached through between two of the rods and retrieved it carefully avoiding knocking the railings which might have alerted the 'thingy'. Nothing grabbed his arm. He stood up and weighed the stick in his hands, then tested it's strength by trying to bend it to see if it would break – it didn't. Daniel smiled.

Safely outside the park railings Daniel's courage was rising. Time to provoke a reaction. He walked slowly along the path which corresponded with the hawthorns allowing the stick to bang on each railing; clang, clang, clang, clang, clunk, clang, clang. At the end of the section he turned around and went back, repeating the operation several times didn't produce a reaction but still he persisted; slow, steady tapping like this always produced a reaction from Angela, and his mom come to that, so it was worth a try. Of course, you had to be careful with provocation – especially when you were messing with Angela, you had to have good reactions, be able to run like hell and hide in an instant. Knowing your escape route helped – in this case it would involve shooting around the corner, throwing himself over a three foot hedge once out of sight, dropping flat and lying very still if something did come for him. He turned one final time and stopped dead nose to belt buckle with PC Helen who had appeared seemingly from nowhere. Daniel didn't think he'd done anything wrong, but wasn't sure.

"Not been near the railway have we?"

"No Mr. Helen," he squeaked truthfully.

PC Helen held out his hand and obediently Daniel put the stick into it.

"Don't want you annoying the residents, do we?"

"No Mr. Helen."

PC Helen casually tossed the stick over the railings behind him. Daniel watched to see if something snatched it out of the air. Nothing did. In retrospect that should have been obvious. The 'thingy' wasn't much bigger than Daniel and therefore much smaller than PC Helen. Plus Daniel thought that something the size of King Kong would probably run and hide in a bush if PC Helen glared at it, so a little green 'thingy' would have to be pretty thick to draw a policeman's attention to itself unnecessarily.

PC Helen patted him on the head, in a way which managed to be mildly friendly and yet very disconcerting at the same time, then stepped around him and carried on with his beat without so much as a backwards glance. About a minute later Daniel started breathing again. When PC Helen was out of sight he began gently tugging the railings until he found the one that had gone 'clunk' when he'd hit with the stick. When he tugged this one it rattled in the top and bottom rails that held it in place. He gripped it and pushed it upwards. The base lifted out of the bottom rail. He squeezed easily through the gap it left and down a slope of a few inches into the park. He wiggled the rail and by twisting the bottom back and forward and digging it into the soft earth a little way he managed to pull it down from the top rail too, freeing it completely. Now he had a six foot spear! If Daniel had known the word "emboldened" then he would have used it to describe his current feeling, but for now a "Yes!" from between clenched teeth sufficed.

He marched around to the other side of the hawthorn bush. He jumped. There it was just as before, a dimly lit tunnel leading somewhere he knew could not exist because he'd just come from the other side of the bushes and there was no sign of it there. The direction of approach that he had used meant that he was closer to the tunnel's entrance than previously and he was to one side of it rather than directly in front. Holding his spear so the spike was about a foot in front of him, meant that it was off balance – too long really for a little boy so he shifted it forward in his grip a little and brought his right arm back to be nearer the blunt end, it was a bit awkward but it meant that he could carry the heavy bar a little easier.

Cautiously he came right up alongside the entrance and peered round the corner, spear protruding in front of him. It was empty, but then it had seemed empty before. He scanned every visible inch but the creature wasn't there. Still cautious he examined the construction of the tunnel walls. They were tightly woven hawthorn and a dim light shone through the gaps between the branches, although 'shone' perhaps was the wrong word, 'glowed' was probably more appropriate, whatever it was it wasn't daylight, more like twilight. There was a smell too. Sweet and earthy, mixed with a musty smell that he recognised from last Autumn, when he, mom and Angela had gone walking in the woods and there had been this smell there then, the smell of mushrooms and fungi growing in the dark damp bits amongst the trees. There was something else too, something he didn't recognise, it was slightly intoxicating, rich and.. He snapped back to alertness, realising he'd been drifting. Quickly he scanned the tunnel again. Nothing. Staying alert to sounds and movements this time he crouched down so he could reach inside the tunnel mouth. He held the spear horizontally in his right hand close to the floor and touched the nearest cobblestone with his left fingertips. It seemed to sing, but the song was felt rather than heard. He put his hand flat on it; the stone was warm to the touch as if someone had been holding it in their hand for some time, not cold as he'd imagined. He lifted his hand away and the singing faded. He stroked the moss between the cobbles and it released a faint perfume. He sniffed it and thought how beautiful it smelled. Next he touched the wood that composed the walls, disappointingly it felt like normal hawthorn but he noted that although the branches weaved in and out not a single thorn protruded into the tunnel; they all faced in other directions.

Because he was crouched down and at the side of the tunnel he saw the creature as it came around the bend a couple of seconds before it saw him. They both froze. Golden eyes regarded him, their wideness matching the wideness of the mouth which had dropped open with surprise below the upturned little nose. Slowly the mouth closed and turned into a smile. Little sharp looking white teeth showed a grin in a green tinged face topped with a shock of dull green hair. Everything about the little man before him apart from the eyes and teeth was green, clothing – a tunic and shorts, skin, the small knife in the scabbard at his right hip, everything, even the wings growing out of his back which Daniel could see over his shoulders. There was no mistaking them. They were like butterfly wings but see-through and tinged – well –

green. He smiled back, this was wonderful! As he did so his grip on the spear slackened slightly and the iron tip gently dropped until it came into contact with one of the cobbles where it made the faintest of 'tink' noises. The creature's eyes popped even wider open, it's hands shot up to cover it's ears and it screamed! A high pitched unearthly scream. There was a snapping sound and Daniel found his face in the hawthorn bush where a moment before there had been open space. He fell backwards onto the grass, gasping from the shock as thorns scratched his face. Panicked, he yelled and thrust his spear into the bush, but there was nothing there. Jumping to his feet he pulled it out and thrust it in another twice to be sure – nothing. He wiped the blood from his face and looked at it on his hand. Only little scratches, nothing major to be shouted at for. He walked back round the trees to the railings and squeezed through onto the road again, with a little effort he got the spear back to being a railing again. A figure in the distance coming along the road looked to be PC Helen returning along his beat. Daniel scarpered before he could be recognised. As he crossed the footbridge over the railway the church clock struck six o'clock in the distance so he put on a spurt of speed; it was at least half an hour later than he thought and he was cutting it fine.

At home after tea Daniel sat at the dining table with his sketch book and crayons trying to capture what he'd seen. He was quite methodical about it. First he drew the little man with wings, which was awkward because he only had one green pencil and he wasn't good at shading. Since the little man was entirely green then what emerged was a green blob with another green blob on top for a head and stick like arms, with the requisite stick like fingers, and legs. Then he did the eyes, but because the yellow would not show very well over the green he licked the end of the crayon which always made the colour richer and scrubbed until there were two yellowy green blobs. He did the same with the red crayon for the nose and smiley mouth because eight year olds always draw noses and lips red even if in real life they are green. Next came the wings which were easy since they were like butterfly wings and any child knows how to draw a butterfly. He looked at it and gradually it dawned on him that what he'd drawn was a fairy. A green fairy. That had thrown him at first since he thought fairies were little people with wings that could land on your hand. This was bigger and greener than the fairies of his imagination but the shape was unmistakeable. He had suspected that it was his mom who placed the ha'penny under his pillow in return for his teeth when the fell out, but his belief in the tooth fairy was now rekindled. Although on reflection the thought of this particular fairy creeping around in his room and scrabbling about under his pillow for teeth as he slept was alarming, Daniel prayed he didn't lose any more teeth in the near future. He wondered if the fairy might decide to take the teeth still in his mouth if it ever turned up and didn't find any under his pillow – if that happened would there be ha'penny?. Perhaps it had a pair of little green pliers in it's pocket for removing the odd tooth from sleeping children. He ran his tongue around his gums to familiarise himself with his teeth – in future he'd check there weren't any missing.

The tunnel was a brown spiral scribble in a horseshoe around the fairy and the two trees were stalks done in the same brown crayon as the hawthorn set either side of the tunnel and green scribble for foliage on top. To differentiate the trees from one another he drew acorns in the left one and winged seed pods in the ash tree on the right. Acorns are a delight to draw. You do an egg, put a line across the midpoint and then criss-cross the bottom half. The ash seeds weren't as much fun but were easier – inverted 'V's with a blob where the two arms joined. His mother often warned him about licking the crayons to get a better colour, telling him he'd be poisoned with them, but all the kids at school did it and they didn't die so he always took the risk. Plants were a different matter; he knew that loads of plants were poisonous if you ate the seeds or seed pods or berries if they were red. So it made it even more exciting to lick the red pencil and draw loads of red berries on the hawthorn arch. There! They looked really poisonous.

There were hawthorn hedges around parts of the school playing field and there was strong argument as to whether they were poisonous or not. Daniel fell into the 'if it's red and you eat it you'll be dead!' camp but Joseph Armstrong maintained his nan made jelly or jam out of them. It was therefore widely assumed that Joseph Armstrong's nan was a witch who would poison you as soon as look at you with her home made jam. The fact that she had a black cat proved it. In the end it was decided that Joseph should prove they were safe to eat by actually eating one himself. If he died then everyone would know they were poisonous. If he didn't die then everyone else would eat one. However, faced with so much expectation that he would die Joseph wouldn't play ball and the matter was never settled. Daniel took up the green crayon again and titled his work – 'The green fairee in the horthorn bush'. Happy, he admired his work for a minute and then closed the sketch book and pushed it to the side of the table.

Chapter 4 -The next day after school

Daniel went back to the park after school the next afternoon. Again he bypassed the gate and after a quick check to make sure he wasn't observed he lifted the railing from it's base, slipped through the gap and dragged it free. Thus armed he trotted round to the tunnel again secure in the knowledge that his spear was sufficient to frighten the fairy if needs be. To his great disappointment there was nothing there, just a mass of hawthorn. He sat down on the grass about ten feet from the bush and contemplated it, his spear stuck in the ground next to him, but it's weight was too great for the depth he had driven it into the soil and it leaned further and further over until he pulled it out and set it down beside him. Nothing happened.

Today was a bit warmer, the wind had dropped and the sun was out. He could hear the birds singing and relaxed, yawning as boredom began to set in. Nothing continued happening for ten minutes or more, he was considering wandering off to find something more interesting but then suddenly and very faintly there was a whirring in the bush, which could have been a bird's wings but probably wasn't. Daniel tensed and waited again. His hand reached down slowly and felt the cold iron at his side; his little fingers wrapped themselves around it but did not lift it from the floor. Minutes ticked by and the whirring came again. Then, very slowly the tunnel started to be there again; it was difficult to see how it happened, if he looked directly at it then nothing seemed to change but in his peripheral vision there was movement of branches and somehow the cobblestones were forming on the floor; he'd forgotten them, he'd draw them in on his picture when he got home. At last the tunnel was there before him complete. He gazed into it and then realised that the fairy was there already, he'd come along the path this time and was just inside the tunnel mouth. Daniel didn't move, he just stared at the fairy, who was staring back, not at Daniel but at the hand which held the spear.

Very gently Daniel said,"I won't hurt you."

The fairy looked at him, there was deep concern all over it's face.

"Are you a fairy?" asked Daniel.

The fairy nodded, slowly at first the faster and faster, it started to grin and then in a slightly comical voice said "Yes, fairy." It stopped nodding and smiling and looked concernedly at the spear again. "We don't like that." it said in a voice which was quiet, and crackled in an odd way.

Daniel got to his feet, the fairy took a step backwards it eyes wider than ever. "It's alright" said Daniel,"I won't hurt you, I just want to show you, it's just an old bit of fence really." he stepped forward to the tunnel and stood a couple of feet from the entrance holding the rail point down. The fairy was trembling

"Please," it begged, "we don't like it, take it away?"

"You have a knife." Said Daniel."It's only fair I have a spear."

The fairy looked distractedly down at the knife on his belt. He waved his left hand over it and said something under his breath – the knife wasn't there any more.

"See.", said the fairy smiling, although very anxiously

Daniel grasped the spear with both hands and drove it into the ground as hard as he could, narrowly missing his foot as he did so, and stepped away from it; this time it stayed upright. The fairy seemed a bit happier, it beckoned him and he stepped forward to the mouth of the tunnel. The intoxicating smell hit him again drawing his scenes in, he smiled and so did the fairy, a lovely smile. Everything was lovely, there was a lovely sound too a ringing of bells, distant though and dreamy. He took a step actually into the tunnel, the fairy was stretching out his hand in Daniel's direction. The bells were ringing again, single chimes this time one, two, three, slower and slower. Daniel stretched his hand out too and started to bring his other foot forward into the tunnel too. Four, five. The bells meant something. Six. Six! It was the church bell striking six! The spell broke. He was late.

"Sorry, I've got to go!" he shouted at the fairy who jumped back in astonishment. Daniel spun and headed back round to the fence grabbing his spear on the way. He fumbled fitting the spear back in it's place but did it eventually and then ran hell for leather back home. As he crossed the road from the park the church clock was ringing the quarter. That was impossible! The tunnel was right by the fence and he'd only paused a minute putting the spear back. Daniel wondered as he ran if the church clock could have broken. He came to the point in his journey where he would have to make up his mind whether to use the pedestrian crossing and risk the fury that would surely descend on him like a pack of ravening wolves if he was caught or, arrive home five minutes later than he would already. He decided to chance the crossing. Arriving there he looked in all directions. No one about. He entered the kissing gate and checked up and down the track. No trains, still no one in sight. He sprinted across the tracks and through the gate on the other side.

"What time do you call this?" said his mother in a raised voice. Knife and fork in hand as he interrupted dinner.
He looked at the kitchen clock on the wall, it's hands betraying the fact that he was almost twenty five minutes late for his food. Someone at school had, to much howling and mirth, mentioned that when asked by their mother 'What time do you call this?' they had replied 'George. Why, what do you call it?' He pondered whether an injection of such wit would lift the situation. He imagined his mom and Angela gasping for breath as they rolled around on the floor, slapping their thighs and laughing at his comic genius. Then he noted that from where his mom was sat her wooden spoon was within reach and he imagined its painful

impact for back chatting.

"Sorry mom.", he said and put on his best 'sorry' face to match his statement – big blue puppy dog eyes and a down turned mouth.

"Dinner is served at six o'clock sharp in this house young man!"

This wasn't strictly true. In the Smith household dinner was served when it was ready although that was normally between six and half-past. He thought better about pointing this out too in spite of the unfairness of the whole situation.

"Sorry mom"

"Yours is in the oven, it'll be hot so be careful." she said putting her knife and fork down and rising from her chair. Behind her back Angela very deliberately and slowly stuck her tongue out at him. Since he was in his mother's line of sight he was powerless to retaliate. As she stepped into the kitchen he turned to make sure she wasn't watching and then spun round and stuck his tongue out back at Angela. She was busy finishing her dinner again, not looking at him and smirking because she'd correctly anticipated his actions. He stamped his foot in frustration just as his mother came back in carrying the plate in one hand which was clad in an oven glove and she promptly slapped him on the arm with her free hand.

"That's enough! Don't you dare come in here stamping your feet when I tell you off. Now sit down and eat you dinner properly and not another word out of you or you'll be going to bed without it!" She set the plate on the table holding it with the oven glove before turning and putting it down on the table to take back into the kitchen later. Angela saw her chance and her tongue came out again. Once more Daniel was beside himself but his mother was back in her place before he could do anything again. He stabbed his fork into the mashed potato, lifted a large lump and rammed it into his mouth.

"Wahhhhhh!"

"For goodness sake! I told you it was hot!" shouted his mother, getting up from her place and going into the kitchen, quickly pouring him a cup of water and putting it down by his plate. Mean time Angela stuck her tongue out once more, screwed up her face and rubbed her eyes as if crying. Daniel was incandescent but powerless. He grabbed the water, gulped at it and it assuaged the pain in his mouth.

"Eat your dinner slowly." his mom said softening and rubbing her hand through his hair to comfort him. Daniel managed a smile. He smiled even more when he got a jam tart for pudding.

After the table had been cleared Daniel went out into the garden. A little bit of digging in the flower border with a stick soon rewarded him with what he was after.

Chapter 5 - The next morning.

Next morning Daniel was out of the back door, closing it as silently as possible and heading for school early and with very good reason. Angela, who attended the grammar school had further to walk than he did and was therefore normally the first of them to leave the house. It was a close thing; he had just closed the door when he heard her squeal.

"Mom! He put a worm in my shoe! The little beast!"

"Daniel! Daniel!", he heard his mother shout and Angela replying, "He's just gone. I'll kill him when I catch him!"

Daniel stood and laughed his head off. He had the common sense to move away from the back door and into the entry passage as the door was wrenched open and a large, flat looking worm was flung into the yard before the door was slammed again.

"Now I'll have to clean my shoe!" he heard her yelling.

Wait till she got to school and discovered that he'd also bent the nib up on her fountain pen, not much, just enough to ensure that it wouldn't write properly without blotting, she could easily bend it back but it would really cheese her off. Better be careful tonight. Angela was a proper tomboy when she wanted to be, she was known to scratch, bite and pull hair when she was angry. In the Junior school one day a lad in her class had tried to look up her skirt and she had battered him; leaving him with a black eye and a nose bleed. He'd told everyone that he'd fallen over in the playground, because no boy would ever live down the shame of having been beaten up by a girl. The teacher in their class, Miss. Fairfield, had a fair idea of who was responsible for what by the looks that passed between them, smug ones from Angela and fearful looks from her crestfallen victim, but she did nothing because Patrick Watts was forever annoying the girls and although Miss. Fairfield wasn't quite sure what he'd done, he probably had it coming to him. Angela was therefore demonstrably more than capable of giving Daniel what for.

Yes, be careful of Angela tonight if she hadn't cooled down, he thought as he came towards the end of the terraced street he lived in and finally stopped chuckling. A door slammed and rapid footsteps clattered on the flagstones of the pavement some distance behind him. He turned casually to see who it was, expecting to see a schoolmate rushing to catch up with him. No such luck. Angela was about seventy yards behind him and closing fast, her blazer flapped behind her and she held her straw boater in her hand. Her face was a rictus – teeth bared, nostrils flared and a dangerous light glinting in her eyes. It was Daniel's turn to squeal, then he ran. The way to school meant crossing the road in front of him but there was no time to check for traffic so he dodged left around the corner into Alma Street hoping for some cover. The road, like all the roads in the area was a continual line of terraced houses, it was empty so he ran along the pavement, checked the road was clear of traffic over his shoulder and then crossed diagonally over the road to the other side, still running all the time. He was aware that he hadn't crossed the road in the way that had been drummed into his skull, and that a horse and cart or a lorry could kill him, but he was also aware that Angela WOULD kill him so the risk was easily taken. He reached the next cross roads and looked back briefly. Angela was nowhere in sight. He paused for a moment, unsure whether it was a trick, but there was nowhere for her to be hiding. Relieved, he turned the corner into Balaclava Avenue and walked down it before turning right again into Inkerman Street, turning left at the end of Inkerman Street would put him back on course for school. Further along the road he could see a girl walking away from him in the straw boater hat of the grammar school uniform, but it wasn't Angela. He walked briskly along about fifty yards behind her, chuckling to himself again about his trick with the worm. The girl in front of him reached the crossroads and looked to her left.

"Oh! Hello Angela." she said.

Angela's head poked round the side of the house at the corner, her eyes searched up and down the street and settled immediately on Daniel who yelped in panic. She'd been waiting for him. He'd been ambushed! Before she was fully round the corner Daniel was halfway back up the street. He was faster than Angela but only just and she had better stamina so in the end he knew she'd catch him unless he found sanctuary. Reaching the junction with

Balaclava Avenue again, instead of turning left back the way he had come, he turned right because it didn't mean losing valuable time, and (probably) life preserving ground by crossing the road again and suddenly realised he was in a dead end heading for the railway. The only way out was the pedestrian crossing at the end of the Avenue. He prayed there wouldn't be a train coming. His little legs were starting to ache now, his lungs were bursting and his throat was rasping. He gained the kissing gate and looked frantically up and down the track. Nothing in sight. He shot through the gate, slamming it behind him so that it clanged and vibrated. Across the wooden sleepers that formed the crossing and through the second gate, slamming that too and then away down the street hell for leather.

"Oh, now you're in trouble! Mom's going to find out you crossed the tracks count on that!" Angela yelled.

He heard the first gate clang again as Angela came through it, then a pause as she checked the track followed by the deep sound of her footfalls on the wood. A second clang indicated she was across the railway and footfalls harder now on asphalt matched Daniel's. There was a clatter, a squawk and a thud, he looked over his shoulder, Angela was on the floor, her right knee bloodied, she'd obviously tripped. Daniel stopped, wondering if he should help her if she was hurt, but grimacing she ignored her knee and started to rise to her feet. Daniel took off again, grateful for the lead that had opened up and for the fact that she'd be slower with a banged knee. A quarter of a mile further on and he was at the park gates, they were both going slower now, trotting, and soon he'd opened up the gap to about one hundred yards. Going in through the park gates was no good, Angela would follow him, find any hiding place he might choose, and then pummel him, so he carried on to the end of the park railings and then turned into Hob Lane. He put on a spurt of speed, as indeed he knew Angela would while he was out of sight, found the loose railing, lifted it and slipped through and pulled it back down so that it slid back down onto the ground. It didn't go into the bottom rail, but sat slightly forward of it, there wasn't time to adjust it because he could hear Angela's uneven footfalls approaching the corner, he hoped it wasn't too obvious. Then quickly he slipped round to the other side of the hawthorn bush, which appeared normal today. Panting he dropped to the ground and sat there with his back to it, regardless of the dew on the grass making the back of his shorts wet. He was hot and sweating so he took his school cap off and dropped it on the ground next to him.

Angela was also hot and sweating, her knee was throbbing too. She had come round the corner into Hob Lane only to find it empty. There was nowhere for Daniel to have gotten through the railings and he couldn't have scaled them. She scanned the tops of them hopefully anyway, but he wasn't impaled there. The houses opposite the park were posh, with driveways and low hedges defining their boundaries, several of the driveways even had cars on them, Austin's and Morris's. He had to be hiding in one of the front gardens, but which one? Then she heard the tolling of the school bell signalling that it was ten to nine. She could just make it on time if she hurried, Daniel would have to wait until tonight before she could sort him. She'd give him worms! She'd hold him down and make him eat one!

"I'll get you later!" she shouted, sure that Daniel would hear her. "You've got to come home sometime! And when you do...". She turned on her heel and limped off as quickly as she could.

Daniel also heard the school bell and realised he would have to go. Then he heard Angela shouting, he wondered if she really was going or if it was a bluff to see if he would come out of hiding. He'd have to look. He started to get to his feet and felt a hand placed gently on his shoulder. He gasped, and spun round and found himself looking into a pair of golden eyes set in a mischievous green face. The tunnel had opened soundlessly behind him and the fairy was standing on its threshold with only it's arm out of the opening. The fairy's face split into a smile and Daniel smiled back, the fairy's eyes were captivating, hypnotic even.

"Come and see." it said, and stepped back into the tunnel, beckoning Daniel. Daniel stood up properly, stepped forward and followed the fairy into the tunnel.

Chapter 6 - Evening. The same night.

By a quarter past six Mrs. Smith was ready to serve dinner and there was no sign of her son. By half past six she was fuming. By seven o'clock she was worried and had sent Angela out onto the streets to look for him, something Angela did with the keenness of a hunter looking for prey. By the time a concerned Angela came back at five and twenty past seven Mrs. Smith was frantic. He'd never been later than half past six. When dusk came at half past eight she put on a shawl to protect against the coming evening chill, and leaving Angela - who had been out twice more with no result - in the house, she walked down the street to the red phone box. There was someone making a call in the box and one more man waiting patiently rubbing two pennies together between his fingers. In spite of the urgency of the situation she hesitated to push in front of the queue and spent five more minutes walking to PC Helen's house. When she knocked on the door he answered in his shirt and braces with slippers on his feet. She told him all she knew, that he had left the house that morning for school and that he hadn't come home and that Angela hadn't been able to find him in the local vicinity. He reassured her as best he could, asked her who Daniel's teacher was at school and the names and addresses of any close friends that he had noting them down in his notebook which he took from his uniform tunic hanging in the hall, then he told her to go home in case Daniel had shown up in the mean time and promised to be round directly. Once she had gone he phoned the police station and spoke to sergeant Richmond who was due to come off duty at ten o'clock, then he put his tunic, belt, shoes and helmet on, checked his note pad and pencil were back in his breast pocket, put his truncheon in his trouser pocket along with his battery torch and handcuffs. Finally he pulled on his long greatcoat and walked briskly to Mrs. Smith's.

When Mrs. Smith arrived home it was dark. There was still no sign of Daniel. Angela had lit the gas lights on the walls, even in the front parlour, which was only normally used for visitors, but hadn't drawn the curtains. When she started to draw them Angela protested that they were open so that Daniel could be sure it was their house if he was lost. Mrs Smith explained that Daniel would know his own house even in the dark and drew them, before putting the kettle on the hob for a cup of tea. She felt that a sense of normality would be better for Angela's sake in spite of the fact that she was beside herself. A few minutes later there was a knock on the door, they both jumped, their hearts' in their mouths', but Daniel would have come in through the back door without knocking and besides that was a knock with authority behind it, not the knock of a child. PC Helen had arrived.

The three of them sat at the kitchen table whilst PC Helen made notes in his notebook. He addressed Mrs. Smith as Edith and Angela as 'sweetheart'. In spite of the terrible feeling in her gut Angela kept looking at the policeman's helmet on the table and in particular at the black badge on the front of it that was worn at night. She wondered if PC Helen had two helmets, one with the black badge for night and one with a silver one for days or if he just swapped the badges over when it got dark. Other equally stupid thoughts filled her head – anything to subconsciously hide the thought that was screaming to be heard.

Eventually she blurted out "It's my fault! I chased him this morning for putting a worm in my shoe and now he's run away 'cos he's too scared to come home!" with that she dissolved into floods of tears. It all came out; the way she'd chased him, the route they'd taken – the railway crossing caused raised eyebrows and more tears from Angela who suspected there might be consequences but knew that the truth must be told. PC Helen calmly noted down Daniel's last sighting turning into Hobs Lane.
"I saw him there a couple of days ago." he said.
"I think he must have been hiding in one of the drives behind a hedge but I didn't have time to look for him. Maybe one of the people who live there caught him and locked him in their house." said Angela.
"He'd found a loose railing there in the park fence by tapping a stick along it, it's odds on he went into the park by lifting it and

dropping it back in. We can start by checking there.", said PC Helen. "I spotted him there a week or two ago. He's not daft."
Angela was stunned, she'd never have believed that her brother was that sneaky to have a secret escape route, and that he'd used it on her. For a moment her hopes rose, but then they fell again as she realised that even if Daniel had slipped her grasp then that didn't really help as he still hadn't come home, and was still missing.

There was a knock at the front door. Angela looked up full of hope but quickly realised that it was again the wrong sort of knock. Mrs. Smith went to get the door and came back with Sergeant Richmond following her down the corridor. If PC Helen was scary then Sergeant Richmond was terrifying. PC Helen and Angela both rose to their feet. Angela stepped back and bumped into the wall behind her. If Sergeant Richmond appeared in your street and you were a kid you didn't hang around you fled. Like the PC he was over six foot, and the slightly faded medal ribbons, including the Military Medal won for bravery, on his chest showed he belonged to the previous generation. Before the Great War he had been a professional soldier, being one of the troops sent as the British Expeditionary Force to France in 1914. At the Battle of Mons he had been one of those British troops who first fought the Germans.

The Kaiser had told his troops that he would send the police to arrest the 'contemptible' little British army, but at Mons they had extracted a hideous price from the cream of the Kaiser's army with a rate of fire from their Lee Enfield rifles unmatched by any other army in the world. There after they had been called the 'Old Contemptibles' and precious few had survived until the armistice in 1918. Sergeant Richmond probably owed some of his survival to a lump of shrapnel that was still buried in his leg from the Battle of Mons, which had meant months recuperating and spared him the fate of many of his comrades who perished in the artillery and machine gun fire of the trenches and no man's land during 1914 and '15.

Sergeant Richmond glanced around the room taking everything in. He briefly made eye contact with Angela whose own red eyes widened like saucers and then he turned to PC Helen.
"What do we know?"
"As far as I can tell, Angela," PC Helen indicated her with the end of his pencil and both police men looked at her, "the boy's sister chased him into Hobs Lane just before nine o'clock this morning where he vanished. I'm pretty sure he's got a rat run through a loose railing in the park fence and he went through there. Either way that was the last time he was seen, so I'm proposing to go straight down there and start looking just as soon as we've finished here, will you be coming with me sergeant?"

Sergeant Richmond looked at Angela and winked – that was quite scary in itself, "What do you think of that Angela? I've got to go and hold my PC's hand because he's scared of the dark." He smiled, PC Helen snorted with derision. "If anything the dark is generally scared of me – or should be if it knows what's good for it." he retorted. Angela had no difficulty believing this, PC. Helen certainly frightened her, although she was starting to warm to him."Don't worry lass, we'll find your brother. First, I think we should see his room, would you like to take us up there Angela." Angela got up and walked to the door in the corner of the room which led to the stairs, the two policemen followed her leaving their helmets on the table. "Mrs Smith, can you come with us? We probably won't find anything but it's important to check for clues just in case."

"Yes of course Mr. Helen." she replied.

Angela was inwardly a little disappointed that neither PC or Sergeant produced a magnifying glass to look for the clues, obviously real policing was a little different from the Sherlock Holmes stories which played at the local Odeon. Instead they systematically checked everything in the room. Starting with the obvious; the contents of the drawers. There was nothing out of the ordinary there. However, pulling the chest of draws out and looking under them revealed a catapult made from a forked branch and a length of knicker elastic which Mrs. Smith recognised as something she had lost from her sewing box, and

56

presumed she had misplaced somehow, and a peashooter made from a thin piece of copper pipe along with a small half empty bag of dried rice.

"What does he want rice for?" Mrs. Smith asked.

"For the peashooter." Replied PC Helen, "The kids like to use it in the picture house. It has a shotgun effect in the dark rather than a straight shot like a dried pea. The usherette is always chucking them out if she can catch them."

"Oh." Mrs. Smith was seeing a new side to her son.

There wasn't anything else in the room of interest. This weeks copy of the Dandy with Korky the cat on the cover was under the bed, along with the normal detritus that a small boy will shove under his bed. Bits of paper, and small pieces of dried and shrivelled orange peel, which must've been there since Christmas. Mrs. Smith squirmed inwardly at the state of the floor under the bed. What sort of slattern would these two policemen think she was? What would they tell their wives about her housekeeping skills? Who would their wives tell? Was Sgt. Richmond married? She knew PC Helen was but was unsure about the Sgt. Why didn't she think to tidy the room before PC Helen arrived? With hindsight she should have known that he'd want to see Daniel's room. If she could have crawled under the chest of draws she would have done.

As they searched they spoke to Angela and Mrs. Smith, drawing out small details. Any rows, apart from the worm in the shoe incident and the pen nib which Angela was fairly certain but not completely sure about? Any possible reason why Daniel would run away or stop out? Places he might go? Who's doors had Angela knocked on – she had been thorough and received praise for that. There were however no real clues in the sparse little room, so after a while they trooped back down the narrow stairs. Once in the back room PC. Helen walked to the table to retrieve his helmet but instead reached forward and picked up Daniel's pencil case. One of those long wooden ones where most of the top half of box pivots when you slide out the lid. He had spotted the gold coloured 'D' transfer on the top which identified it as Daniel's, he opened it and removed all the coloured pencils, the rubber and the pencil sharpener that it contained. There was nothing else so he put everything to it's rightful place. Then he picked up the notebook under it and leafed through it. With Sergeant Richmond looking over his shoulder. He paused when he came to the picture of the fairy in the hawthorn bush, but neither he nor the sergeant said anything

"Good evening Mrs. Smith – we'll let you know directly we have any news." Said the sergeant, and with that the two policemen left.

They walked briskly through the streets and across the railway lines. They briefly checked the lines for the bits and pieces of flesh and other body parts which would have been spread up and down the track for many yards if a small boy had in fact come off second best with a locomotive. In truth someone would have noticed and called the police if something had occurred so they carried on towards the park talking in quiet tones as they went. "I don't like this Bob" muttered Sergeant Richmond.

PC Helen looked at him. "Nothing to worry about yet surely?" he said in a tone that said he was no longer quite as sure as he had been. "Gut instinct?"

"Maybe. Maybe I'm getting old, but this doesn't feel right. How far up Hobs Lane is that rat run?"

"Not far, just a few yards. There's a couple of trees in the corner of the park with a tangle of bushes around it – just past that."

This time the sergeant turned his head and looked at the PC, then he looked straight ahead and quickened his pace. PC Helen did likewise. They turned the corner into Hobs Lane and both began shining their torches along the park fence. PC Helen drew his truncheon held it loosely in his left hand and trailed it across the railings producing a rapid series of clangs. Sergeant Richmond, slightly ahead of him reached for the railing he had spotted which was still out of place and lifted it. PC Helen shone his torch through the gap. "Someone's definitely been through here." he said, "See the snapped grass stalks? Looking withered – that was done quite a few hours ago. We're not going to get through that gap – let's go round."

"Learn your tracking in the Scouts did you?"

"I was a Scout." said PC Helen, "but I learnt to do this hunting Jap in the jungle with the Chindits."

"Oh." said the Sergeant impressed. 'Oh.' was about the greatest expression of being impressed that he ever used. PC Helen was secretly pleased.

The park gates were locked so they walked a little further and forced their way through a larger gap in the fence which had never been repaired – it was still a tight squeeze for the two large men. They walked back towards the two trees shining their torches on the grass as they went. Bumps on the ground and twigs cast long shadows and as they approached them.

"There!"

They stopped as the torch picked out Daniel's school cap lying on the floor a couple of feet away from the hawthorn patch. The grass here was short and springy and therefore not much use for tracking. They scanned the area with torch beams before the sergeant went forward squatted and looked inside the cap illuminating it as he did so, then he lifted it so as to read the name written in ink on the label. It read 'D. Smith'.

PC Helen walked forward and squatted along side the sergeant. He put his torch, which was the size and shape of a chunky hip flask with the bullseye lens where the screw cap would be, flat on the floor and pivoted in an arc. As he did so little pockets of shadow a fraction of an inch deep showed themselves. He traced them carefully with his index finger. "Heel marks from a child's shoe." he said with confidence. Keeping the torch flat he moved it forward still pivoting it at the same time picking out more of the marks in a pattern that lead towards the mass of hawthorn.

"That's funny," he said, "there's no marks coming back – could he have forced himself into the bush to hide from his sister? Dan? Daniel! Are you in there? DAN?" He forced his arm into bush thrusting the torch in and twisting it round trying to illuminate the interior without much success. He pulled it out snagging his uniform coat on the thorns.

"Maybe he crawled out around the side." he said and began moving round the hawthorn crouching and twisting his torch again. "He definitely went in there!" He looked back at the sergeant who hadn't moved and was still shining his torch at the patch of Hawthorn.

"Come on sarge! Help me look for crying out loud."

Sergeant Richmond looked like he was in a dream but he snapped back to normal as soon as he was spoken to and he began imitating PC Helen's actions with his own torch. They circled the patch in opposite directions and met on the far side.

"Nothing. You're sure he went in there?"

"Yes Sarge. I've found his tracks as he came through the fence and towards the place where he dropped his cap, but nothing coming out of the hawthorn patch."

"Right. Check the side I've just done in case I missed something."

A short while later they stood back where they had started from.

"He MUST still be in there." said PC Helen.

Sergeant Richmond whipped the shiny metal whistle on it's chain out of his top left tunic pocket put it to his lips and blew hard – long repeated blasts. PC Helen did the same with his whistle, in his case a wartime pattern black Bakelite one. After a few seconds there came an answering blast some way off followed by another one fainter and therefore further still. Sergeant Richmond stopped blowing and spoke.

"Bob, go and rouse the neighbours get them to bring garden shears over here, we have to get into that mess."

PC Helen moved off with a turn of speed which more than one fleeing criminal had been surprised at. Sergeant Richmond went back to his whistling.

Within a few minutes the two police men, who had been summoned by the whistles of sergeant Richmond and PC Helen had arrived and quickly joined four local men hacking and pulling at the hawthorn with a variety of gardening implements. It was harder than it seemed coordinating things in the dark with four small hand torches. Actually rakes worked better than shears as the larger branches were too thick to cut. PC Helen gradually forced his way into the bush at the point it seemed that Daniel had entered. He cursed as branches and thorns whipped and tore at him. It wasn't a big patch, just a few yards by a few yards, but it seemed to him that he was back in the jungle. He slowed up and went at it more methodically directing the men with the rakes to pull branches and twigs out of his way. He crouched down shining his light around him. Four yards in there was a hollow area. Sunlight didn't penetrate in here so while trunks and branches grew up through it there was no foliage and it was possible to see the interior clearly with the torch. The dry floor was littered with dead branches but very little else apart from an empty pop bottle. It's top had been smashed off so that some child could get at the marble trapped in a cavity in the neck which kept it sealed, before throwing into the hawthorns, but apart from that the area was undisturbed – no-one had been in here for some time.

PC Helen worked his way through the interior on his hands and knees shining the torch in all directions and peering into the shadows which danced across the entangled branches. From the other side another constable, PC Humphries was forcing his way in and the beam from his torch gave a sense of direction. It became obvious after a while that there was no-one, alive or otherwise in the hawthorn patch apart the two police officers. Reluctantly they withdrew by backing out, their uniforms snagged and their knees pierced by hawthorns. PC Humphries was clutching something in his hand.

"This is all I found he said" holding up the rusty remains of a horseshoe. " It had been placed in there deliberately by someone resting it upright against a brick end but it hadn't been disturbed in a long time."

He looked at it in the torch beam and then deciding it had no real worth and not wishing to be carrying the unnecessary weight of a lump of iron around for the rest of his shift he tossed it gently towards the hawthorns.

"Is there anything else we can do sergeant?" This was from one of the locals.

"Well if any of you has torches we will conduct a search of the park, while you're fetching them check your driveways and front gardens, actually if there's access to the back gardens check them too including coal holes, w.c.'s, sheds and shrubbery – anywhere a small child might have squeezed. Check your neighbours property too, let them know what you're doing first though and see if they can help search too. Broom stales might be handy for poking in vegetation – but not too hard mind, I don't want young Dan skewered. Just a thought, this is a mining area, it's just possible a hole has opened up, so tread carefully and work in pairs so we don't lose anyone."

The neighbours dispersed back to their houses to find such torches as they had and to denude the household brushes of their heads, to the mild chagrin of their wives.

"Constable Littleton, you'd best check the perimeter of the park from the outside, check under the hedges and so forth, but before you go, see that bush about fifty yards to your right?"

Without moving his head, the fourth officer on the scene, PC Littleton's eyes swivelled to the right, found the offending bush, paused for a few seconds and then swivelled back to the sergeant.

"Yes Sergeant."

"There's been a courting couple watching us from there since we arrived. Go and sort them out."

Littleton smiled. "Yes sergeant." he turned and marched towards the bush.

"You pair!", Littleton shouted.

There was an answering female squeak of fear from the bush, followed by a male groan of resignation.

"What are you up to? – no don't tell me I can guess. There's a law against that sort of thing, you filthy, grubby little devils!"

Chapter 7 – Fairyland

Daniel was still following the fairy, following and being pulled from time to time now, they had left the tunnel some time ago, Daniel wasn't sure about how long ago though, the tunnel hadn't seemed very long so they hadn't been in there that long had they? His head said a couple of minutes, but his feet said it was miles; they were aching now and he felt tired. The strange intoxicating smell didn't help either, he found his thoughts fuddled slightly. There was someone he was supposed to see, or was it somewhere he was supposed to go? There had been something, something that served as a reminder for something, but he couldn't quite remember; then for a moment it struck him, a bell – the school bell!

"Whoa! I'm going to be late for school", he said and came to a halt.

The fairy stopped too and looked at him with a mix of incomprehension, and petulance.

"We don't care about school, it doesn't matter here. You will see."

"What will I see?" asked Daniel

"Wonderful!" said the fairy

"What do you mean, wonderful? Wonderful what?"

"Things."

"Wonderful things?"

The fairy nodded vigorously. "Come, you will see wonderful

things."

"You sound like Howard Carter." said Daniel, who was keen on his Egyptology and knew that when Howard Carter broke through into Tutankhamen's tomb and stuck his head inside he reported, upon being asked what he could see. "Wonderful things."

The fairy had never heard of Howard Carter, Tutankhamen or Egypt, but he nodded anyway. "Yes."

"Are we going to see a Pharaoh's tomb?", said Daniel.

The fairy thought about it and nodded, "Tombs. Yes – there are tombs to see, who told you that? How did you know?" It looked puzzled.

"I know about tombs," said Daniel, and because he also knew about curses placed on tombs by Pharaohs, he carried on, "And I ain't going in one no matter how many wonderful things are in it. Don't you know about the curses?"

The fairy looked aghast. "Oh, we know all about curses, we are good at curses, you will see. Now, you will come with us!"

"No, I'm going to late for school, I'll come back to the tunnel tonight after school if that's alight and we can chat."

He turned around and noticed for the first time that he was in a forest – the tunnel was no where in sight, just this deep, dark and rather scary forest of spindly, green trunked trees, rich with moss but rather lacking in leaves other than the tiniest dark green offering which hung sparsely on the branches. Where was the tunnel? How long had he been in the forest? He had been that intent on following the fairy that he hadn't noticed his surroundings. His head felt strange, so he shook it and looked around again. As he looked he saw a faint trail of a path leading back the way they had come. As in the tunnel there were cobblestones but they were more overgrown, harder to spot and much more sparing in their frequency. He started to walk back the way he thought he had come, slightly hesitantly because the trees seemed menacing. The thought of what might become of him if he arrived late for school was more menacing still though. There was a screech of rage from behind him and the fairy grabbed him by his jacket sleeve and tugged hard.

"You come with us!"

Daniel pulled, the fairy pulled harder. "You will come with us!" it shouted.

Daniel swiftly unhooked his leather school satchel from over his head and shoulder with his free arm and swung it hard by the strap. It caught the fairy round the side of his head, he screeched, more in surprise and indignation that pain, but let go and fell backwards grabbing at the satchel.

Daniel let the fairy have the satchel and showed it a clean pair of heels as he fled into the forest along the path. He couldn't run as fast as he'd run from Angela because his feet were aching, he felt tired and the path, such as it was, was uneven and somewhat vague, however the fairy didn't seem to be following him as he looked over his shoulder, breaking the first law of being chased by something.

He stopped for a moment to get his breath and his bearings. There was no sound of wind in the woods. He looked at the trees. They might be described as saplings by the width of their trunks but they stretched high and seemed to bend over the path blotting out whatever passed for the sky. Whatever the sky was here didn't resemble the normal sky much. Dull, green and overcast without any visible texture or cloud. This wasn't any sort of place that Daniel would have imagined fairy land. The atmosphere was dank and oppressive. He tried to peer into the trees looking for some sign of civilization or humanity, but he could only see a few yards in any direction. Then something not too far away, but still hidden in the trees growled. Daniel ran again. When he stopped, he was panting and out of breath. He listened hard above the hammering of his own heart and the gasping of his own breath, there was nothing growling or even moving, but he could hear water trickling nearby. Realising he was very thirsty he pushed into the trees. The thin trunks moved with effort, but there was little or no undergrowth. He moved a few yards further and came to a small clearing which he hadn't been able to see from the path. There was a carpet of small dead leaves on the floor, they were moist and squelchy underfoot, around the edge of the clearing were little clumps of mushrooms or toadstools – he couldn't tell which and wasn't about to go near them. At one side of the clearing there was a small rock face from which water tricked into a small pool rimmed with rocks. From a gap in the rocks a small stream flowed out slowly and disappeared into the forest. The water looked dark and slow moving in the pool and stream, but the water from the rock looked fresh enough. He walked forward and knelt as close as he could get. Then he stretched his arm out cupping his hand. The water was colder than he imagined. He moved his hand to his mouth and tried some – it tasted delicious and refreshing, he took more and more until his thirst was satiated. Out of the corner of his eye he saw something reflected in the pool, something that moved fast, far too fast to be identified. He whirled round looking about wildly but everything seemed still and nothing moved. Time to move on, he hesitated, which way? He hadn't crossed the stream and the stream bisected the clearing so if he turned and faced away from the stream and walked into the trees he should hit the path, shouldn't he?

Chapter 8 – Talk of Angels

"Alright, thank you for your help gentlemen you can go home now." - this was sergeant Richmond to the neighbours. They walked off talking in a little group wishing the police officers good night."
Disappointingly the search had produced nothing. They'd covered the entire park from end to end, but in fairness apart form the corner with the hawthorn patch and it's immediate surroundings there wasn't much to hide a small child for very long. There were low, well clipped ornamental hedges over the other side of the park dividing the flower beds. and the play area. Apart from that there was a large flat area suitable for football matches if you didn't mind the large and small mud baths located all over the pitch and especially between the two goal posts. Sgt. Richmond didn't care for the feel of the mud under his feet. It bought back memories of the Somme, he fancied he could still hear the thump of guns and smell rotten corpses in his nostrils. He'd forced those thoughts out of his head to concentrate on the job in hand, but his feet still placed themselves carefully to avoid imagined stray strands of barbed wire, and the squelching torsos and body parts which had lurked in the hell of Flanders.

"Right." said the sergeant when the civilians who had helped with the search had gone homeward. "I'm going back to the station and phone headquarters, there's nothing else to be done here tonight. Humphries you'd better go straight there and sort your uniform out – you look like you've been dragged through a hedge backwards."

"Yes sarge!" said PC Humphries with a grin on his face.

"Right Bob, just before you get off home." Sergeant Richmond held up Daniel's school cap. "I have to ask. Are you sure it's there that he went into that patch?"

PC Helen pursed his lips and looked away embarrassed by his failure "I was. I'd staked my life on it to be honest. I guess I'm not as hot at tracking as I was in Burma. I'm sorry Sarge."

"That's okay Bob. You did your best. Do you know the history of this little patch of the park?"

"History? No."

"When I was a lad a young lass went missing. She was last seen in this park, she was never found but when they searched the park a child's skeleton, thought to be a little lass who'd disappeared about fifty years previously was found."

"Do you know where about it was found?"

"Right here I believe."

PC Helen was silent. A chill went up his spine.

"By any chance was the little lass seen by these bushes?" he said after a while.

"I can't say for certain, but she was a bit of a loner and didn't have many friends. She had a bad squint and we took the mickey out of her." He pursed his lips, "She talked about fairies a lot – I suppose if you're a kid with no friends you make them up. After she'd gone we said she was away with the fairies. You can be very cruel when you're a kid. Funny how it can come back to haunt you." He pursed his lips again.

"Do you think that horseshoe could have been put there like a memorial Sarge? I saw it when Humphries picked it up off the brick, there were two twigs there too but they crumbled when he touched them. They'd been tied in the shape of a cross."

"Rowan." Said the sergeant.

"Rowan, as in the wood – mountain ash?"

"It wasn't a memorial Bob, it was left there by Emily's – that was the little girl's name – her cousin I think. Iron horseshoes, rowan wood and crosses are all supposed to defend against evil. She put it there after Emily disappeared. She was a little bit older than us, she still lives in Tylers Road. She believed in fairies too, and she put the fear of God into us."

"You don't believe in fairies do you Sarge?" This was said with a tone which managed to convey the impression that if the answer was 'yes' then the sergeant would never hear the last of it.

PC Helen couldn't see the Sergeant's eyes in the shadow cast by rim of his helmet. None the less, he felt them move to look at him. The sergeant turned his first his head and then slowly his entire body in the same direction, so that they were face to face and almost toe to toe. Bob Helen wasn't intimidated as many men would have been, but he recognised the intent.

"Have you ever heard me speak about the war Bob?"

"No Sarge".

Sergeant Richmond was talking about the Great War, like many men who'd been through either world war he rarely, if ever spoke about his experience. "I know you were in before it kicked off."

"You've heard of the 'Old Contemptables'?"

"You were one of them?" Said PC Helen with awe in his voice.

'Don't worry about the contemptible little British army' Kaiser Wilhelm told his vast army, 'I'll send the police to arrest them all!' He had every reason to believe his own words. Britain had 380,000 troops compared to Germany's five million.

"I was at Mons," said the sergeant, "We lined up on the side of the of the Mons-Condé Canal and waves of Germans appeared on the other side. They came marching up out of the forest on the other side of the canal, totally unaware we were there until we open up en-mass and cut then down in waves. We'd have held them too if they hadn't driven school kids across the bridge in front of them. That and the fact that the damned Frogs withdrew from our flank leaving us exposed, so we had no choice but to withdraw ourselves, but during the battle I saw the angels of Mons with my own eyes. So to answer your question 'Do I believe in fairies?' I know angels exist, so let's say I have an open mind on the subject," he took one slow, measured pace forward, so that they were now really toe to toe and stared from under his helmet at PC Helen, his eyes were still invisible but PC Helen couldn't avoid the feeling of them boring into him. – "and if you ever mention this to anyone else folk'll think Joe Steptoe got off lightly the other month."

"Yes Sarge" - Ye Gods! Did he know about that?

"Go on clear off home, there's nothing can be done tonight. We'll start again in the morning."

"Yes Sarge."

Chapter 9 - Fairyland – the cave of mirrors

Finding the path wasn't as straightforward as it might have seemed. The trees seemed thin enough to see through, but in reality Daniel couldn't seem to see more that a few dozen feet, by rights he should have been at the path sometime ago, but he seemed to have missed it. How could that be? A path is a straight line, surely he should cross it at some point? Then, he came to another clearing at the base of a small cliff about twenty feet high. There was a cave about the height of a man at the bottom of cliff. He stared at it for some time. Daniel liked caves. Well he'd never been in a cave or even seen one in real life so it was more accurate to say that he liked the thought of caves. There was treasure, cavemen and dragons in caves—suddenly that didn't sound so good—were dragons real? He was sure they weren't but then what about fairies, a few days ago he'd have said no. Bears on the other hand—bears were real, he knew that for definite, and bears lived in caves too. He'd read enough comics to know that too. He didn't think there were bears in England—well not outside of the zoo anyway, but was he still in England any more? This fairy country, was it part of England or was it a magic realm? That seemed more likely, so bears were a possibility, and so were dragons for that matter. He decided to bypass the cave and skirt round the edge of the clearing keeping an eye on the dark opening in case anything came out of it. About halfway round he stopped—there was a light in the cave and it looked out of place. It wasn't like the dull green light of this place; it looked warm and homely instead. Summoning up all his courage Daniel debated entering the darkness to investigate. On the plus side bears didn't use lights and it didn't look like a flame as you'd expect from the nostrils of a sleeping dragon—it was too steady and didn't flicker like a flame. Also it didn't look remotely fairy in that it wasn't green, more the white light of a gas lamp in a house. That might mean people, but if it did then what sort of people? Good or bad? On the down side was that it was still a cave and although he liked caves he'd never actually been in one. He wished he'd had his spear with him from the park railings. He looked down at the mossy forest floor and his eyes fell on a stick; not a big stick but something at least. He stripped the fine branches from it with his hands and finally held something about three foot long and more like a school cane than a spear – still, better than nothing.

He advanced cautiously to the cave entrance swishing his stick at some of the sickly looking plants which grew through the moss, snapping them off. Finally at the entrance, heart pounding, he stood and listened – the silence was deafening. He picked up a pebble from the ground. Looking in he could make out several more lights of various intensities, they gave the impressions of gaps in the wall with light showing though, like the rusty piece of corrugated iron that he and some friends had found and used to make a den on the waste ground behind the park last summer by curving it over and driving sticks into the ground along side to peg it. It had been six feet long and about eighteen inches high like a tunnel and therefore not really much of a den as dens went. It was fun to crawl through and to look through the little holes without being seen.

He threw the pebble into the cave and heard it rattle as it landed and bounced along the floor. Nothing happened. A thought struck him. What if it wasn't a cave? What if it was actually another tunnel made of stone instead of hawthorn? Could it be a way home?

He stooped and this time picked up a handful of pebbles which he flung underarm into the darkness. The resulting clatter made him jump, but once the stones had finished rattling there was silence again. Stick in hand he advanced into the cave. The floor was uneven and the lights some distance in, so he quickly started using his stick as a walking stick feeling the way and thus making staying upright much easier. At one point he found a pit, how deep he couldn't tell but a couple of feet at least. He used the stick to probe around and find a safe path at the edge of the cave. His feet found a small stone and he kicked it sideways in to the pit, the was a brief pause and then it hit the floor – not bottomless then, but probably several feet. The floor smoothed out, feeling like the cobblestones of the hawthorn tunnel and he made better progress,his spirits buoyed by the thought that it might indeed be away home. There were no more pits and walking steadily and carefully he finally came to the first of the lights, he approached it and was shocked. It seemed to be a window of some sort and on the other side was;

"ANGELA! ANGELA!" she was sat at the table in the back room, she turned in her seat and he could see her eyes red and face all tear stained, but she wasn't looking at him. From somewhere out of sight of the window PC Helen appeared helmet in hand, Daniel realised that he must have come down the passage from the front door along side the front parlour. Daniel's mom followed him. "MOM! MOOOOOOOM!" he screamed, but it seemed that no one could hear him. He couldn't hear them and they couldn't hear or see him. They were talking and his mom and Angela were wringing their hands and crying. Their shoulders moved with occasional sobs. He smashed his stick against the window in an effort to break it and then used it to dig out one of the cobble stones under his feet, he snapped the stick but had made a hole into which he could dig his little fingers and get some purchase. A stone came loose, he pried it free and hurled it as hard as he could at the window. As he did so he brought his other arm up to protect his face from the expected shower of broken glass. He'd broken several windows with stones in his time and knew what to expect. The stone, the size of a rather squarish cricket ball, bounced off with a dull thud and didn't even chip the window. Daniel stood watching his family through the window for some time. Sobbing with them and pressing his little palm against the glass, or whatever it was, in an attempt to be nearer to them. It dawned on him that he was looking into the room from the mirror on the wall. It's oval shape confirmed that view. At last he stepped away and walked towards the next light. Another mirror he guessed. Oval again but longer rather than wider this time. Through it he saw a man and a woman, again they were sat at a table, but the clothes they were wearing seemed strange and old fashioned. The woman's skirt was almost touching the floor and the sleeves of her blouse were loose on the arms and tight at the cuffs. Her hair was swept up in a bun. The man's legs were hidden by the table but his collar stood up against his neck and his face which was gaunt had mutton chop whiskers down the sides. The woman was weeping and the man appeared to be trying to comfort her. She picked up a framed sepia tinted photograph from the table, Daniel could make out a girl with long curling locks and notably cross eyes.

The third window was tiny and showed a small room lit by a single candle. There a man sat again at a table with a dark bottle from which he drank. It was difficult to see much else so Daniel moved on.

The next window was larger and squarer. Daniel thought that if this was a mirror then it must have been expensive, the view of the room through it tended towards that. It was a large room with a marble floor in black and white checks. A staircase, grand and quite wide was against the far wall. Beside it was a chaise longue upon which a golden coloured top hat rested on it's side. A man in a red jacket and mud spattered long boots strode to and fro. His eyes wide and his hand running repeatedly through his hair in a distracted fashion. In his hand was a riding whip. Another man approached in rougher clothes, also spattered with mud. He approached with a look of despair on his face. The first man listened to him speaking and then turned from him and slashed at the top hat with his whip sending it flying. He covered his face with his other hand, presumably to hide his tears.

Daniel stepped away and looked for the next window. The cave turned through ninety degrees and he realised that to follow the line of lights, and there seemed to be a lot of them, he would lose sight of the cave entrance which he was loathe to do. He walked back to the window on his own room and watched again with tears trickling down his face. Once again Angela seemed to be alone, then she turned and PC Helen and his mom walked in again. So, not a window, more of a film show like at the cinema repeating over and over. Not Angela, PC Helen and his mom, just images of them, but so real looking. He started to walk back towards the entrance of the cave and kicked something which rolled along the floor. He stooped and picked it up finding it to be the stone that he'd previously dug out of the floor. He weighed it in his hand and then shoved it into his pocket, with his stick gone he lacked a weapon, this might do until he found another suitable stick. Unfortunately without his stick he also had no way of finding the pit before he fell into it – which is exactly what happened.

Daniel was light enough not to seriously hurt himself when he landed but he was winded and scraped and sore all over. Standing up he realised there was no way he could reach the top. The walls were smooth rock which gave no purchase for climbing and there was nothing but moss patches on the floor, which may have cushioned his fall, but were of no use to man nor beast for climbing out. Desperately he felt round the walls all to no avail. He pulled the stone out of his pocket and smashed it against the wall, producing a few bright orange sparks but little else. After a while he put the stone back in his pocket slid down the wall to a sitting position, slid his feet up underneath himself and started to cry.

He wasn't sure how long he sat there, but eventually the tears stopped and looked up. On the ceiling of the cave were two small golden lights a few inches apart. And then they blinked. Daniel gasped and froze. They blinked again and straining hard Daniel could make out the familiar outline of the fairy. He could also make out it's grin and the sight filled him with rage. There was no way he was going to beg to be let out so he sat and glared at it. There was some movement and something fell into the pit and slapped against the side of the pit. Daniel raised himself to his feet and stepped across the pit - his hands found a rope. He thought about it for a moment and having weighed his options tugged on it and found it was secure so he reached up and started to pull himself up it as he would in the gymnasium at school. As he climbed he plotted, he couldn't grip the stone and the rope at the same time so it was still in his pocket, but the moment he was out of the pit he would pull it out and bash the fairy with it. He wondered if he could throw it into the pit, but realised that it would simply fly out. He wondered if was strong enough to pull it's wings off like a fly's but he doubted it. Then he was at the top and pulling himself over the rim. A hand gripped his hand hard and a loop of rope dropped around his wrist, was snapped tight and used to yank him out of the hole with considerable force. There was a hiss of triumph from the fairy and a yelp of shock from Daniel. The fairy pounced on him and they rolled back and forward perilously close to the pit Daniel reached for his pocket and the stone, but his free wrist was grabbed and forced up behind his back. In seconds the rope was flicked around that wrist too and then it was a simple matter of pulling the rope and his two wrists were drawn together and swiftly bound.

"See if you can run off now!" shrieked the fairy.

Chapter 10 – Mons 1914

Bill Richmond was sleeping – badly. Sometimes he dreamed of the war – four years of fighting gave you plenty to dream about for the rest of your life. Dreams that often lead him to wake sweating and shaking from the cold, dreams that sometimes he woke from screaming. Sometimes he saw German infantry advancing out of the clouds of yellow mustard gas - in that one he was manning a machine gun – a Vickers, a belt fed beast of a weapon. Beautifully engineered, not known to jam or fail. Sat atop it's tripod it would spew out the best part of five hundred rounds of ammunition per minute for as long as you held the spade grips, pressed the safeties off with your thumbs and gripped the triggers with your fingers. Except when he had this dream the gun wasn't working – it was firing, it just wasn't having any effect on the figures shambling towards him out of the yellow mist with their bayonets reaching towards him, their faces hidden from view inside their gas masks. Tonight it was a different dream though, this time he was reliving actual events rather than experiencing a terrifying fantasy.

He was looking out across the canal at Mons from a trench, the Great War wasn't yet a month old and the British Expeditionary Force, including Private Richmond had just had it's first contact with the enemy that very day, the air was thick with the smell of burnt cordite, the propellant used in British bullets. Smoke hung above the battlefield from the sheer amount of firing which had taken place, despite the fact that cordite was officially smokeless. Troops along the line of the shallow trench, in their khaki uniforms, replete with puttees wound like bandages up to their knees and peaked caps on their heads were cheering and jeering the Germans who had retreated back to the forest on their side of the valley between attacks leaving dead and wounded thick on the ground behind them. The cheers of the men were mixed with a constant noise of moaning, punctuated by screams from the wounded and dying of both sides.

An officer, identifiable by his brown boots up to his knees and his beige twill trousers dropped down into the trench beside Bill pistol in hand; he had been taking a chance standing up away from any cover, but officers sometimes felt they needed to prove something to their men or perhaps themselves, or perhaps it was to thumb their noses at the enemy. This one, Captain Hythe, was quite excited. "Look up men, what can you see? What can you see?" He pointed a hand in fine brown leather glove skyward.
"They look like.." Bill stopped short and rubbed his eyes.
"Do you see angels men?"
No one spoke, reluctant to say that they could see angels, and yet looking up high in the sky were golden shapes which looked awfully like angels.

Captain Hythe, a tall, slender man still the right side of thirty, with a waxed moustache which was beyond his years, didn't seem bothered with his men's reaction. "Private Richmond. Take a message back to the HQ, would you?" Although phrased as a question it was still an order. As a company runner it was Bill's job to take messages to and fro, dodging enemy fire and ensuring that important information flowed smoothly.

Captain Hythe held out a folded scrap of paper.

"Sir? Are you reporting the... Well, are you telling HQ that you can see angels?"

The Captain looked at him shocked and then grinned. "Goodness no! They'd have me in a straitjacket before you could say Jack Robinson. I just needed to be sure that I'm not seeing things. This," he waved the paper, "is just a report to say that we have driven off another attack and that our casualties are moderate and morale is high and could we have some more bullets please because the Huns seem to intent on us using them all on them."

"Oh," the troops grinned and chuckled.

"What do you think it means sir?" one of them asked.

"Well, they're above our lines, so I think God must be on our side – as he always is being an Englishman - Angels are associated with Christmas, so my guess is that it's a sign that the war will be over by Christmas."

Grins all round again. Someone waved at the angels – they didn't seem to wave back. Bill pocketed the note. He took several deep breaths to oxygenate his system, pulled his cap down a little tighter on his head and made sure his webbing was all secure. Then he checked his rifle was loaded, gripped it tight, clambered out of the trench and set off at a sprint as fast as he possibly could. Half expecting an enemy bullet at any moment gave him wings and he ran as fast as he ever had in his life. He could hear the banter behind him.

"Use your binoculars sir, see if they are waving back."

"I don't have any binoculars with me or I would."

"Wonder if I could hit one from here?" Private Steptoe's voice. There was a discharge from a rifle, and a shocked silence followed by the sound of a loud smack to a head and a yell of outrage from Steptoe.

"What the cowing hell was that for? That hurt that did!"

"Shut your filthy trap in front of an officer you little guttersnipe! Discharging a weapon without an order – you're on a charge Steptoe!", that was Corporal Smith. "Aiming a weapon at an angel – what're you trying to do? Bring the wrath of God down on us? You idiot! You complete idiot!"

"Take cover!" shouted Captain Hythe.

There was a whistling sound which grew in intensity and a German shell landed and exploded a couple of hundred yards away. Bill lowered his head and somehow ran even faster, better the wrath of the Kaiser than the wrath of God, despite his fear he chuckled at Steptoe getting a thick ear off the corporal.

If anyone was going to do something childish, mean, stupid or irritating it was Steptoe. Everyone in the platoon hated him for the trouble and extra duties that he generally brought down on them. It was water off a duck's back to Steptoe, he just didn't care. More shells whistled in and he felt the concussion from one. Bill had been holding his cap onto his head with one hand, but in order to run faster he let go and it immediately bounced off and he lost it. Peaked caps looked grand on the parade ground but were pretty useless for the purposes of modern battle, he let it go – he had more important things to worry about. The shells built into a storm of fire and steel. Bill's legs were going like pistons on a locomotive, his heart pounding like a steam hammer and his lungs burning like coals in a furnace; still he pushed himself on, ignoring the agony of sprinting for hundreds of yards. The shells were missing the trench but bursting on the ground behind them. Bill was nearly at the edge of the forest and the fancied safety of the trees when almost inevitably a shell came for him, the whistle changed to a deafening scream and he threw himself flat, eyes closed, mouth open to help with the massive over pressure which would follow the detonation. He dropped his rifle and pushed his fingers into his ears praying it would be a dud. He didn't hear the explosion, but a giant hand lifted him from the ground and threw him cruelly many yards. A searing, burning pain burst into his thigh and he tried to scream – impossible because the pressure forced the scream back down his throat. An eternity passed and he made contact with the ground again bouncing and cartwheeling along it like a rag doll.

It went quiet. Was he deaf with shock? Out of the dust and smoke a figure approached, a bright golden white figure, so bright that Bill couldn't understand how he wasn't blinded by it. He reached out a hand and opened his mouth to yell for a stretcher bearer, instead he beheld an angel.

"I'm dead!",he whispered to himself, and then in panic "What will my ma say?"

The angel stood a couple of feet away from him and looked down at him. He could see shells still bursting and debris flying about, but the gleaming white robes of the angel moved as though in a summer breeze not a maelstrom of screaming death, not that Bill could hear any screaming, or anything else for that matter.

"Why me?" he asked looking at the angel. "Why me?"

The angel knelt and looked at the wounded leg. Bill wasn't sure whether he heard or felt the response. "There is a purpose to it. One day your prayers will be answered and then you will understand." The voice was like a roaring waterfall, or rolling thunder in the distance, full of power.

He thought he must have felt it because he still seemed deaf to everything else. "I'm not dead am I?" he asked hesitantly.

"No."

"Am I going to die? Please don't let me die in a hospital."

"I don't tell fortunes." said the angel without a trace of humour, rising to his feet.

"It was Private Steptoe that shot at you, he's always been a wrongun. I knew him back home."

"I know who was responsible – he wasn't the first to try."

"As long as you know it wasn't me, I not trying to get him in trouble or anything. Hey, you are still on our side though aren't you? And the war will be over by Christmas?"

The angel didn't answer him, instead a single tear trickled down a face so perfect that it could have been carved by Michael Angelo. The angel looked upwards; wings, huge white gleaming wings extended sideways from his back and he was gone. Bill couldn't tell if he flown upwards or simply vanished, but at that moment he entered a world of pain as the shrapnel wound in his thigh made really itself known, and after screaming at the top of his lungs he passed out.

Chapter 11 - The dressing station

In 1949 Bill woke with a start, and sat on the edge of his bed for a while thinking uncomfortable thoughts. In 1914 Bill had also woken with a start, his hearing had returned, and there was a thumping pain in his thigh. A nurse in a grey uniform with a white headdress and apron with a medal on the right side (to show her nursing qualification rather than her bravery), passed the end of the bed that he was lying on and seeing he was awake paused and asked how he felt?

"Did they take my leg off?" He blurted out.

"No. Just a flesh wound. It's small but deep so they've decided to leave the shrapnel in place. Once it's healed properly you should be fine." She said quietly. She was young and pretty and although he felt rough, sympathy form a pretty girl made him feel better.

"Bill." A voice made him turn his head to his right, there in the next bed was Private Steptoe looking at him. "Bill." he repeated weakly, then lay there still looking at him.

"Steptoe, nice to see a friendly face." Bill replied although he didn't really mean it. Steptoe just lay there looking at him. After a minute or so the nurse moved to Steptoe's head, blocking Bills view of him. She spoke a couple of times calling Steptoe's name, lifted his wrist to take his pulse and finding none closed his eyes and pulled the sheet up to cover him.

She turned to Bill, "I'm sorry. Your friend's gone." she said softly.

"Oh," said Bill. "Nurse? What killed him? was it a bullet or a shell?"

"I think it was shock," she replied, "there wasn't a mark on his body. When he spoke to you it was the only words he'd spoken since he arrived here. At least he had someone he knew with him when he died."

"He shot at an angel.", said Bill and immediately regretted saying it.

The nurse gave him a strange look. "Try and get some rest Private, we're going to have to evacuate in the next hour or so. The French have broken and we're exposed, our lads have no choice but to retreat from Mons and the Huns won't be far behind them. We're trying to organise wagons for the wounded now. Get some shut eye whilst you can." and with that she walked away.

In the distance Bill could hear the dull rumble of a constant artillery barrage, he looked about him, he seemed to be in a church crypt. An awful lot of beds seemed to have been placed in the available space. Here and there were oblong tombs, some flat topped, some with reclining effigies of the dead lying on top of them, the effect was surreal. There were no windows and for light electrical bulbs had been strung along the stone walls. They weren't sufficient on their own and large candles, presumably from the church, burned at intervals. Bill looked around, suddenly he felt sweaty and cold. A monk in a full black habit stood at the head of bed a couple of rows in front of him. His hood was raised and he stretched out a hand towards the bed's occupant, the hand appeared thin and bony, in fact it appeared almost skeletal. A nurse walked up, and ignoring the monk checked the patient's vital signs. She stood back a second and then pulled the sheet up to cover his face. She shuddered and walked on briskly. Bill noticed the monk was holding a staff, no wait, it had a scythe blade on it, what was a monk doing with a scythe in a dressing station? He struggled to sit more upright feeling incredibly dizzy. As if sensing his gaze the monk turned his head to look at him across the room and Bill looked back into the skull face of the grim reaper himself, hollow, black eye sockets twinkled with malicious glee, despite the lack of eyeballs, and the teeth, oh my – the teeth! Death turned towards him completely and began purposely crossing the room with a slow measured pace, the end of his scythe's shaft tapped on the stone floor with every pace he took. Tap, tap, tap. The tapping echoed loudly round the crypt. Death grinned at him and Bill heard him chuckle, a deep rattling noise that filled his ears and filled his head . No one else seemed to notice. Death came forward inexorably making a bee line straight towards his bed obviously intent on claiming his immortal soul. Bill looked round for help, still no-one had noticed the black clad fiend deliberately treading a relentless path towards him. Bill made up his mind that if this was it, and his time had come he would meet his end with bravery and show no fear, then his nerve went and he screamed and fell out of bed in wild panic. A nurse was there in a flash, kneeling and muttering soothing words, "There, there, it's okay you have a fever, let's get you back into bed shall we?"

The ground trembled from an artillery shell that had crept a little closer than the others. Death loomed over the top of the nurse, grinned at him in a hideous fashion and proffered a hand. Bill shrieked and shied backwards, he felt the stitches in the wound on his thigh burst and blood began to trickle onto his leg as it oozed past the shell dressing.

"He's come for me! he's come for me!" He tried to push the nurse, who was blocking his view of the oncoming Death, away.

Another nurse appeared with a syringe and there was a painful prick in his arm. Shortly after a sedated Bill was dragged and lifted back onto his bed, grey, shaking and sweating profusely.

Father François, who was doing his bit to comfort the wounded and dying, watched the nurses staunch the bleeding and change Bill's dressing. He pulled the hood of his black Benedictine habit down, crossed himself and muttered a prayer for this English soldier, and wondered if he was in fact a protestant and if so would his prayers be appreciated – ah well, all God's children. His arthritis was playing him up in his hip, so he leaned on his staff wandered on to do more service to the dying. This one he thought would probably live, but there were plenty who would not see another dawn and they must take priority, he pulled his hood back up and limped off, his staff tapped on the floor as he did so.

Briefly he wondered what Bill had seen in his delirium that had alarmed him so much.

Chapter 12 -The retreat from Mons

Two days later Bill sat next to the wagon driver wrapped in a blanket and shivering from cold though his head still felt hot. The worst of the fever had passed, but he was still weak and a little woozy. He was glad that his leg was in a fit state to allow him to sit here. In the wagon itself men were lying groaning with every rut and bump in the road. Every now and again he caught the whiff of gangrene from one of the lads lying there. It's sickly sweet stench turned his stomach. Behind the wagon every so often a drop of blood squeezed between the boards and dropped onto the road surface with a tiny spat.

He didn't say much, he knew he had been delusional for two days or was it three. He had no memory of being loaded onto the wagon, but this morning his fever had lessened and he had managed to climb to the bench seat beside the driver who steered and drove his two horses as gently as he could in deference to the wounded in the back. In reality there wasn't a great deal for him to do, in front and behind there stretched a long line of assorted wagons and ambulances. There hadn't been enough room for all the wounded to be put in proper ambulances so he with many others had ended up in a vehicle purloined from a French farmer along with the two chestnut horses. They were nervous, the smell of burning was in the air and as the column of wounded passed one way a column of troops passed the other way, Marching troops, cavalry with sabres at their sides or lances in their hand, and motor vehicles – taxis and omnibuses straight from the streets of Paris and other cities, all loaded with soldiers, British in khaki and French in dark blue coats and bright red trousers. The French had obviously yet to understand the importance of concealment which the British army had learned some time ago when they ditched their scarlet tunics in battle for clothing the colour of dust which blended better with the surroundings. The French cavalry that passed had shiny helmets and breastplates which gleamed like beacons, they looked fantastic. Bill wondered if he'd have done better in the cavalry, mounted on a charger. He'd seen a squadron of British lancers gallop past a while previously, scattering the infantry off the road before them and guessed they would put the fear of God into the enemy with their wickedly sharp, gleaming lance tips pointing skywards and fluttering red and white pennants.

Overhead an aeroplane droned. He'd seen one before, back home before the war started, and stared at it with an interest he couldn't rouse for anything else in this condition. The infantry marching on the other side of the road looked upwards, they had spotted it too, and they fiddled nervously with their rifle slings. That would just about settle things if they decided to engage it with volley fire – the horses would bolt across the fields that lay at the side of the road. The aeroplane was low enough to see the pilot and observer looking down at the stream of troops, but there was no indication as to which nation it belonged to. Bill thought it might be helpful if aeroplanes flew a flag behind them like battleships.

The aeroplane moved on unmolested and Bill's eyes dropped back to the ground. His leg was throbbing but at least he knew it was clean and uninfected, and at least he hadn't had to have it amputated – unlike the poor beggar with the gangrene in the wagon behind him who would have to face the loss of a limb if he survived the ride to hospital.

Out of the corner of his eye he noticed a poplar tree lying by the side of the road. It appeared to have been hit and knocked over by a stray artillery shell. Beside it was a body, a small body the size of a child. He rubbed his eyes. The tree was peppered with shards of steel shrapnel and another shard shaped like a small boomerang was sticking out of the body's chest, which like the rest of the body was green; he'd almost missed it because it was partly hidden by and blended in with the poplar's foliage. As the wagon moved slowly past he studied it. Bare to the waist with a green skirt or kilt supported by a belt with a dagger and a small pouch. The eyes were closed and the mouth drawn back in a rictus to reveal a row of small sharp teeth. Underneath it was a pair of butterfly like wings, translucent, now crumpled and broken.

"No....!", Bill's eyes were nearly popping out of his head. Was this another hallucination caused by the fever? He genuinely couldn't tell any more. He screwed his eyes up, opened them and looked again. Still there. He was suddenly transported back fourteen years when he was a small child.

Chapter 13 – 1900 - In the witch's lair

That day fourteen years earlier, he had been in Miss Ball's class. She was an ugly old spinster, whom rumour had was a witch. Certainly the wart on her nose and the besom, or broom stick, that resided beside the fireplace in her classroom seemed to confirm that. All the children in her class were scared of her – she had a quick temper and a short whippy cane, which to their disgust was only ever used on the boys; girls might be shouted at but never had to hold out their hands to feel it's sting. Of course the girls were quite happy with the arrangement, and they did give attention to any lad who had been caned by stroking the vivid red lines across their hands after class and sometimes kissing them better as their mothers did for little knocks and grazes.

Miss Ball was currently out of the classroom and Billy had taken the opportunity for mischief. He walked up to the black board on it's easel as bold as brass, picked up the brand new and unused stick of chalk with a triumphant flourish and pocketed it before walking back towards his desk, pausing to spin the globe, with it's large areas of pink showing the vast extent of the British Empire, on the way. The rest of the class reacted in different ways; his mates grinned at him and he grinned back, certain of the more impressionable of his peers gawped at his sheer bravery, wondering where on earth he got such courage. The rest just ignored him and quietly got on with their work, writing on their slates. The door started to open suddenly and Billy slipped behind his desk just in time not to be noticed by Miss Ball. He picked up his own small piece of chalk and slate, which was noticed and noted too, as was the still slowly rotating globe. Miss Ball had been a teacher for a good many years and knew all the devious tricks that little boys think they are the first to try, so she cast her eyes around her class room to see what had been moved or altered. She started with her tall oak desk which unbeknown to her pupils was left with items deliberately touching each other so as to make it easy to see if anything had been interfered with. The desk draws were locked so she knew Billy hadn't taken a swig of the gin in the small bottle she kept at the back of the top draw for those days when the stresses of the job were a little too much. Next she visually swept her chair for tacks left on the seat and the board to see if anything had been rubbed out or added for humorous effect. Almost immediately she noticed that the new stick of chalk was missing – a little too obvious that particular trick.

"William Richmond. Come here boy." She snapped in a voice that could probably make a bulldog put it's tail between its legs and run for cover.

Billy's heart jumped into his throat. She couldn't know he'd done anything. He left his desk and trooped out to where she stood looking as innocent as he could.

"Yes Miss Ball?"

"Give it.", she held her hand out, palm uppermost.

"Give what Miss?" the faintest note of panic was present in his voice but he was still determined to bluff it out.

Her hand grabbed him by the shoulder and pulled, turning him through ninety degrees before her claw like fingers shot into his trouser pocket, rummaged around and came out clutching the chalk. Billy went red with embarrassment.

"Little thief!", she hissed.

There was nothing for Billy to say. He dropped his head. Miss Ball put the chalk back in the little trough on the bottom of the board and then walked across to the wall where the cane was hanging on a nail by it's crook. She took it down and turned to face Billy swishing it in the air to hear it's whooshing whooping noise. Billy tried not to flinch.

"Well class, it seems we have a nasty little thief in our midst, a viper in our bosom. Some of you may be thinking that I am being harsh to use such language, after all it is merely a piece of chalk, not worth a 'hapeth, but I will tell you this. If young Richmond will take a piece of chalk then why not a bag of sweets from the pocket of a coat in the cloakroom? Why not apples from an orchard?"

At this point Billy blushed even redder than he was already and he wondered if Miss Ball knew all his guilty secrets, and if so how did she know? Maybe she really was a witch and watched her pupils in a crystal ball or the perhaps in the bubbling liquid in the cauldron that she surely had at home for boiling toads and newts in.

Miss Ball continued her tirade. She was in full flow now and had warmed to her subject. "Why not money or a bicycle? Further more apart from theft, young Richmond has attempted to make a monkey out of me! He has breached the trust which I set upon you all when I left the room."
Billy's little heart sank to his boots. It had been a joke, he wasn't a thief just a practical joker, everyone did that didn't they?

"Hold out your hand boy." she snapped, Bill obeyed, knowing to hold out his left hand so that his right hand wouldn't be too sore to write with. He also knew from past experience to move his thumb out of the way so as to avoid the absolute agony of the ratan cane striking the thumb bone. The cane swished down without warning before he could move his thumb and he gasped and hissed, shaking his hand which he clenched tight. Tears sprang from the corners of his eyes.
"Put that hand back."
Slowly he did so, moving his thumb this time and observing the bright red weal already forming like tram lines on his palm. The

cane whipped down again and crossed the first line. Billy avoided yelping, but only just.

"Put your hand back."

Billy complied, his hand shaking and twitching in anticipation.

"Hold that hand still young man."

The cane whistled down and involuntarily Billy pulled it out of the way.

"If you move that hand again William then you'll get extra – take your punishment like a man!"

Billy held his shaking, stinging, throbbing hand out again and closed his eyes in order that he wouldn't move. She brought the cane down really hard, it crossed the other two stripes and this time Billy did yelp. Tears were now making the way down his face

"Sit down."

"Yes Miss. Thank you Miss. Sorry Miss." he snuffled, and returned to his seat, without making eye contact with any of his classmates who having stopped to observe the spectacle of a public execution now recommenced work with a vengeance lest Miss Ball decide she should exercise her caning arm some more. With his sleeve he cuffed the tears away.

"Hasn't your mother given you got a hanky?"

"Yes Miss."

"Then where is it?"

"In my pocket Miss."

"Well perhaps in future you could use it instead of your clothing you little guttersnipe.!"

"Yes Miss."

Billy made a supreme effort of will and stopped crying and resisted the overwhelming urge to snuffle the snot in his nose back up where it came from. He wasn't going to give the wicked witch any more satisfaction. He wanted to wave his injured hand in the cooling air, but instead clenched it as hard as he could in an effort to make the pain go away as fast as possible.

With the chalk returned to the board, the miscreant returned to his desk and the cane returned to it's nail everything was once again in order in Miss Ball's little world, and she returned to her perch behind the desk from where she surveyed her charges from on high.

Chapter 14 – Billy's Revenge

By the time his class had been dismissed for lunch, Billy had hit on a plan. Once out of class he ran across the playground and round behind the back of the toilet block in the corner of the concrete yard noting the large clump of nettles at the far end and dodged through the gap in the hedge which formed the boundary of the school property with the meadow next door. He ran quickly back to his home, literally just across the field from the school. He clambered over the low back wall of the yard of his house and quietly opened the unlocked back door. He could hear his mother talking and guessed correctly that she was on the front door step talking to a neighbour in the street. He shut the door before the wind could catch it. And snuck through the house and up the stairs from the back room, carefully avoiding those treads which he knew would squeak when stepped upon. In the room where he shared a bed with two brothers he opened the top draw in the chest of draws and feeling around at the back he found his most prized possession – a sheath knife. Since his trousers were held up by braces he lacked a belt so he tucked it, in it's plain leather sheath, securely into his waist band where it was hidden by his jacket. He looked at his left hand, still throbbing and a bit painful. Then with a practised move his right hand shot under his jacket and came out with the knife. The handle was made from rings of hide threaded onto the tang and stained dark with use. The six inch steel blade was a dull colour but the edge glinted. He scraped his thumb across it and confirmed that it was sharp enough for it's purpose. He smiled and put the knife back in it's hidden sheath, checked his jacked pocket for the handkerchief which his mother insisted he should always carry despite the fact that he always used his sleeves to wipe his nose. He would need the handkerchief for this piece of revenge. Then as quietly as he had come he went again and returned the way he had come. His mother was still talking on the doorstep and never heard a thing. This time his mischief went unnoticed and he was soon back in the playground with the other kids.

At four o'clock the bell went and Miss Ball dismissed her class. They spilled out of the door in an un-orderly fashion and most of them headed out of the gates. A small gang of boys gathered in the playground just inside the gates. Billy joined them and asked what they planned to do.
"Go to the park for a game of hide and seek?" suggested Jonathan. This seemed agreeable to everyone.
"I have to nip home first. I'll meet you there in a few minutes." Billy said, "Is anyone watching, I'm going to cut through the hedge and across the field?"
Everyone looked around in a fashion guaranteed to arouse suspicion, but there seem to be no teachers about so Billy once again shot behind the toilet block but instead of disappearing

through the hedge this time he went straight to the nettles which were standing about four feet high. He wrapped his handkerchief carefuly around his still painful left hand so that it was totally protected and gingerly and cautiously grasped the nettles near their base. With his right hand he drew his knife and started to saw at their tough stems. That didn't work terribly well so he began slashing at them, very shortly he had a handful of nettles. Checking that no-one was watching him he moved back into the hedge to make himself less observable and settled down to wait.

The toilet block consisted of several individual cubicles each of which housed a wooden box at the far end with a hinged lid, beneath which was a seat with a circular hole cut into it. Waste dropped through the hole and into a large tin container. At the back of the block where Billy was now hiding were a series of small doors which allowed access to the tin boxes. Every so often a 'honey wagon', or more correctly a dung cart, would arrive at the school, a man with a shovel, who accompanied the cart would empty the waste from the boxes onto the back of his vehicle, and would thence convey it to the local farmers where it could be used to fertilise the fields. Not only did he service toilets such as those at the school but also cess pits and earth closets. It was an occupation which normally took place after dark so as not to offend the noses of the local population. Not as common as it once was due to the introduction of water closets, it still provided a surprisingly profitable but none the less lonely existence.

Miss Ball was a creature of habit. Everything in her classroom was ordered and the same was true in her private life, everything had a time and a routine, that was how she liked it. She habitually rose at seven in the morning, and then in strict order went downstairs to clean out the fire in the range and to set the new fire. That done she performed her ablutions in the scullery, returned upstairs, put in her false teeth, dressed and then went downstairs for breakfast; which every morning took the form of a round of toast with marmalade and a cup of tea. These routines went on throughout the day, and it would have been possible to observe Miss Ball's actions at any moment and set one's watch accordingly. Her bowels were no exception to this rule - this was to be her undoing.

At 10 minutes past four, once her class room had been ordered and checked Miss Ball left and headed outside to the toilet block as she had been observed by Billy and many of the pupils to do every day after school. She entered the third cubicle, reserved for female staff, as she always did and bolted the door. That was Billy's cue. He waited for a minute or two until he was sure that she was seated and then quietly he stepped forward out of his hedge. Nervously he opened the back door to the cubicle. The stench was horrific, but he had been expecting it and held his breath so that he didn't give himself away by gagging. He thrust his nettles through the gap between the top of the tin box and the bottom of the seat aiming for the middle where the hole would be. He felt a resistance and rubbed the nettles back and forward vigorously. He was rewarded by an audible gasp and a shriek of pain and terror that any railway locomotive would have had difficulty in matching for volume with it's steam whistle, followed by several more of ever increasing volume and pitch. After a few seconds he heard a door flung open somewhere and footsteps running across the playground. Time to go. He dropped the nettles and ran for the hole in the hedge, finally letting his breath out and bursting out laughing as he sprinted across the field, moving hell for leather and heading this time for the park, unwrapping his hand and putting the handkerchief in his pocket as he ran. He'd been very careful about that wrapping so as not to get a sting. He knew the entire school would be read the riot act tomorrow and that a nettle sting would be evidence of the perpetrator of the atrocity and therefore tantamount to a death sentence. He was still laughing when he arrived at the park a few minutes later for the game of hide and seek. It hadn't started yet but Sam Jenkins had already been selected to be it. He faced a tree and started counting to one hundred.

Billy found a nice tussock of grass near the corner of the park. It was a good position; being close to the edge of the park it was not possible for someone to sneak up from behind, Billy had a commanding view of the area, but his attention was suddenly focused on one small area a few yards away, actually it was focused on a person? Creature? The game took in the whole park and apart from Sam who was doing the seeking no-one else was visible. Sam was at least a hundred yards away and looking in a different direction. The little green man who Billy was watching was watching Sam from another patch of tall grass. He hadn't noticed Billy less than twenty yards behind him. Sam ran off, away from them in the direction of a stand of trees in search of his quarry. The little green man stood up and walked with a strange high stepping motion towards the clump of hawthorn that grew between the big oak and ash trees. Billy could clearly see the wings on his back, protruding through his clothing, folded together like a huge butterfly. He could see that it's clothing seemed to be shorts and a tunic with patch pockets, and a belt around his waist with a knife on the left hand side. It's head was bare with a shock of dark green hair which looked even to Billy, who was not normally noted for any degree of sartorial elegance, like it would benefit from a comb. Suddenly the little man snapped round and looked Billy's direction, his tiny upturned nose twitched and little golden eyes searched back and forward until they rested on Billy hidden behind his grass tussock and peering through its blades. His expression, until now slightly fed up looking, changed immediately; he smiled brightly and invitingly –

albeit through sharp pointed white teeth. The wings on his back stretched out sideways, blurred, whirred and in a bound he was a couple of feet from Billy. He dropped onto his belly and regarded Billy nose to nose through the thin veil of grass. Billy gasped. He could smell the creature, a musty slightly damp but not unpleasant smell.

"Don't be afraid, not going to hurt you, we must be friends, what is your name."

"Sam." Lied Billy. He didn't know what he was dealing with and wasn't about to be disadvantaged by this creature knowing who he was. Lying came easy to Billy, not for nastiness sake but he'd worked out quite early on that he was good at it and that it could save you from a thrashing. Well sometimes it could.

"Sam. Sam come with me – I will show you wonderful things."

Despite his scepticism there was something soothing and even mesmerising about the voice and those golden eyes like sovereigns.

Billy looked across the park, Sam, the real Sam that is, was in the far corner, he had Jonathan Birt with him - obviously he had been found. He looked back to the fairy. Was it a fairy? What else could it be? What could be the harm? But what about the game? Sam would surely see him.

"Come on Sam."

The fairy was looking back and forward between the hawthorn patch and Billy in an agitated way.

Billy looked back and forward between the fairy and Sam. Perhaps there was a way to follow the fairy and stay hidden at the same time. Carefully he got up onto his hands and knees and crawled towards the fairy keeping as low as he could so as not to be seen by Sam. The fairy looked puzzled for a second but then giggled and danced in the direction of the hawthorn patch.

Once they reached it's edge he crouched down close to Billy again. "Watch." it said. Then it pulled out it's knife from its scabbard. The hilt was green like almost everything else about him and it was topped with a smooth rounded clear green stone, an emerald perhaps? The blade was a coppery colour, dull apart from the edge which glinted wickedly and showed it was sharp. He pushed it out in front of him into the mass of hawthorn. Slowly, over the space of what seemed to Billy about a minute a hole formed in the vegetation. It was difficult to see what exactly happened because it was so slow, and if he stared at one particular point then nothing seemed to happen there – just vaguely, in the periphery of his vision, but at the end of it there was a tunnel who's length seemed too long to be contained in the hawthorn patch. There was a cobbled path in the tunnel and moss grew between the stones.

"Come on Sam."

The fairy moved into the tunnel. Billy looked over his shoulder to see if the coast was clear.

"Come on Sam."

Billy looked back at the fairy and didn't like what he saw. The smile was gone and it was replaced by a snarl. Billy, still on hands and knees went to move backwards, but with the speed of a striking adder a sinewy green arm shot out and a sinewy green hand, or possibly claw, grasped Billy's wrist yanking him forward onto his stomach with surprising force. Billy found himself being dragged along the cobbles by a grinning fiend who was excitedly waving a copper bladed knife in it's free hand. Well two could play at that game! He reached under his jacket and his fingers found the handle of his own sheath knife. It was a tool for whittling sticks, sharpening pencils, cutting nettles and the like, not really a weapon, but it would do just fine for the latter purpose. He managed to free it without pulling the leather sheath out of his waistband and he now had four inches of sharp steel that he swung inexpertly in a broad arc which the fairy almost avoided, it caught in the patch pocket of the fairy's tunic and ripped it clear. None the less, to avoid the blade entering his body the fairy had to release Billy.

"Noooo!" it squealed, "Not in here! Not iron!" It swung back with its own knife wildly, hissing through it's teeth and missing.

Billy, on his stomach, instinctively realised he needed to gain his feet he dropped his elbows onto the ground and drew his feet up under him in a jerk and sprang upright into a defensive crouch. The hob nails in the leather soles of his shoes caught and scraped the cobbles throwing out a small shower of bright orange sparks, the noise they made was drowned out by the scream of pain, terror and rage that came from not only the fairy, but which seemed to fill the tunnel and come from it's walls and floor at once. Instantly the fairy vanished as if he'd never existed and the hawthorn snapped shut on the tunnel. Branches and thorns whipped at Billy, trapping him. He had instinctively raised his arms to protect his face and the thick woollen clothing that he wore protected him from the worst of it, but it was still terrifying. He yelled at the top of his breath. Still in a crouched position he was able to push up and partially stand. He'd had the gumption to hold onto his knife and attempted to slash the twigs and branches, but found that a small knife is not much good for that particular job; nowhere near sharp or heavy enough to cut through the bendy twigs.

He yelled again. "Help! Help!"

"Found you!", Sam's voice came from behind him outside of the hawthorn.

"Get me out! I'm stuck!" Yelled a panic stricken Bill

Sam, Jonathan and another lad, who appeared to have been found, George Hope, all pulled and ripped at the twigs. "Keep still Billy. You're not helping by pulling the other way."

Billy tried to keep still and stop panicking and a few minutes later enough shrubbery had been cleared to allow Billy to step back and begin pulling away from the plant life.

He noticed the material from the pocket was still caught on his knife, so unthinkingly and still shaky he pocketed the pocket and put the knife back in it's sheath.

"Blimey," said Jonathan, "You should've stayed put, he'd have never found you."

"How did you get in there in the first place?" Asked Sam.

"Never mind how did he get in there, how did we get him out? It was like the plants were trying to hold on to him deliberately like." said George, which of course made Billy feel a whole heap better – not that he mentioned it.

"What am I going to do with my clothes?" He wailed, "Mom will kill me – again!"

"Again?" asked Sam, "How can she kill you again – are you already dead?"

"No, not yet, but I probably will be, she gave me what for when I tore my jacket the other day falling out that apple tree in the Vicar's orchard."

"Did she know who's tree you were scrumping?"

"Trying to scrump you mean.", Said Sam, "The apples aren't ready yet!"

They were joined by Albert Sturge who had become bored watching the drama unfold from whichever clump of grass he'd been hiding behind.

"Did the Vicar catch you?" he asked.

"Nah, he saw me and came out of the vicarage but I scarpered over the wall before he could recognise me." Said Billy.

"Found you!" this was Sam to Albert, who ignored him.

In the end he went back with George to George's granny, who managed to smarten Billy up with a flannel and some carbolic soap and then also smarten Billy's clothes up enough to make him presentable enough. She worked quickly with a stiff brush and wet sponge to remove dirt and stains. She hung his jacket by the immaculately blackened range in her back room to dry. As she worked the boys explained about the game of hide and seek in the park and how Billy had become stuck in the hawthorn patch. He left out the bit about the fairy, it seemed so strange that he almost doubted that it had ever happened. Then she found some rich fruit cake in a tin and cut a slice for them each, put them on china plates (not the best china of course – little boys tend to drop things like that.) and disappeared with them in to the pantry under the stairs. When she came back she had buttered one side of the slices and she presented it to the boys.

When they had finished eating the cake and picking the crumbs off the plate by pressing the tips of their fingers down on them she took Billy's jacket, checked it was dry with the back of her hand. She slit off the odd lengths of pulled thread with an old cut throat razor which had belonged to her late husband. Finally George threaded a needle for her, his eyes being 'younger' than hers and she deftly sewed a couple of small tears.

"There, good as new!" she declared eventually. George beamed with pride at his granny's prowess at turning an urchin back into a presentable child – a skill George himself had made use of more than once before.

Billy grinned, because unless he fell in a puddle or something daft on the way home he would be spared his mother's wrath. "Thank you so much Mrs. Hope." he said.

She smiled back, then put out her hands to both lads, "Come here and listen the pair of you." she said gently.

"Please stay away from that hawthorn patch in the park." she said once she had a hold of them both by their hands, "It's a bad place."

"I will Mrs. Hope." Said Billy, who had no intention of ever going near the place again.

"Why is it bad Grandma?" asked George.

"Well, it's always had a bad reputation round that corner of the heath, well, park now I suppose it is, but it was a heath when I was a lass. Even the name of the road at the back of the park. Hobs Lane? 'Hob' is an old word for the devil. A young girl from our school went missing about fifty years ago, Enid they called her, lovely little thing with golden locks and big blue eyes. I can see her now. They never found her alive or dead, but that was the last place she'd been seen crossing the common back home from school. It killed her poor old dad. He'd lost his wife a couple of years previously and crawled into the bottle after she died. They found him dead a couple of winters later. Dead from the cold, he spent all his money on booze and not on firewood you see. In truth she probably fell down one of the mine ventilation shafts – they didn't tend to cover them in those days and all sorts got tossed down there – but there was always something queer about that patch and when they searched in the hawthorn they found bones."

"Wow!" said George. "Was it her skeleton?"

"No, I just said they never found her didn't I? Among the ribs they found a couple of buttons, silver ones mind. The old folk thought it was the son of the old marquis who disappeared on a hunt when they were little. His horse came back but he didn't. They'd searched high and low for him and the marquis had posted a reward, but nothing was ever found of him. Well not until they found the skeleton, eventually the marquis put up a memorial in the church. They moved it when they built the new church. Have a look on Sunday, you can't miss it, it's the big white marble one just behind the font."

"I will Mrs. Hope." said Billy, who had gone noticeably paler.

Chapter 15 - One Week Later. - A terrible error

The next day at school Billy's class were lumped in with Mr. Hawkins' class whilst the register was taken. They then marched in their usual lines to the main hall, where the headmaster stood in his flowing black robe and motarboard hat behind the oak lectern. This was unusual, as the classes normally filed into the hall and stood in near silence awaiting his arrival. Billy felt nervous and wondered if it showed. The teachers stood around the perimeter in silence glaring at the children, who apart from Billy, really hadn't got a clue what was happening. When the hall was full, the headmaster surveyed the assembled multitude, doubtless wondering where the miscreant he sought was hidden. Then he opened his mouth and bellowed. It was difficult to hear some of the words through his rage but the gist of was that Miss Ball had been assaulted in a most appalling, disgusting and unmentionable way. He was appalled that one of his children could ever behave in such an un-English way, whoever had done this was no better than the savages who lived in the darkest most uncivilised parts of the world- those parts outside of the Empire. He had never heard of such a vicious act and he was minded to thrash the entire school until their backsides were bloody, one by one in alphabetical order to be sure that the perpetrator was suitably punished. If anyone heard so much as a whisper of a rumour about who might be responsible they were to come to his office straight away and report it, the police apparently were also interested in finding, and speaking to the offender. If the offender themselves came forward and faced their punishment then he would be lenient. With that he turned on his heel and stormed out of the hall, his gown flowing behind him. Billy's face was bright red, he wondered how no one had noticed. He'd tried to keep his head hidden behind the kid in front and not make eye contact with the enraged Head Master during his tirade.

The pupils who had being standing closet to the lectern during this outpouring of vitriol wondered if it was safe to wipe away the specs of spittle from their faces which had streamed from the headmaster's frothing mouth and managed to avoid the filter of his formidable black beard.

In truth whilst he had wondered if he had enough canes, and energy to punish the entire school, the conversation he had had with the local bobby PC Grisdale, had brought enough doubt into his mind to prevent that particular action. He noted that PC Grisdale smelled strongly of spirits and despaired of the perpetrator of this assault ever being bought to book by an officer of the law who had a liking for the bottle. The PC had pointed out that the hole in the hedge meant that anyone could have come through onto the school grounds and perpetrated the assault. Miss Ball had plenty of ex-pupils, some of them now adults, who might feel they owed her a bad turn. Still, he was optimistic that shaking the pupils as one might shake a ripe fruit tree might cause a plum to fall into his hands.

All said and done he still felt that there was a good chance that one of her present class might either be responsible or else at least have some useful knowledge, and for that reason when Billy's class returned to their class room they had a rude shock, Mr. Ramsey would be taking their class; Mr Ramsey who was also known as 'Headmaster', and heaven help the first child who played up.

A week after the incident of the nettles in the toilet Miss Ball had still not returned to school, she was said to be suffering with her nerves. Mr. Ramsey was still taking her class. Getting rid of Miss Ball had been an unexpected bonus for Billy, gaining Mr. Ramsey had been a terrible, and completely unforeseen consequence. Billy had given serious thought to repeating his trick on the headmaster, but he noted that the day after his ambush on Miss Ball the nettles had been cut down. A couple of days later they heard sawing and hammering from the playground. Even if the children had been brave enough to stand on a chair when Mr. Ramsey left the room, as he did periodically, which none of them were, they would not have been tall enough to see out of the high windows so they had to wait until play time. When they went out it was observed that there was now a large wooden gate in the process of being fitted across the gap between the toilets and hedge by a joiner. Once compete it would be padlocked. The hole in the hedge had also been made impassible with a section of fencing. That was one activity which would not be easily repeated.

Billy was standing with his face covered by his hands facing the wall of the school. He was counting. He and his little gang were playing hide and seek again, hopefully this time he wouldn't end up in a hawthorn thicket fighting with a knife against a crazy little green man with wings on his back. A few yards away he could hear 'Cross-eyed Emily' who appeared to have found an audience who'd never heard her stories before.

Emily was talking to some of the younger girls in the playground. "Yes, I had tea with the fairies in my garden last night. We use the tea service from my dolls house. They invite me into their house at least once a week although I'm sure I could go without an invite any time I liked, it's just that in the presence of royalty it's manners to wait to be invited. I was bought up with good manners. Mater insists on manners at all times."
"Are they royal?" Asked one of the little girls who was listening.
"Oh yes, not all of them are obviously, but the King and Queen of all the fairies live in their golden palace under a mound at the

bottom of our garden. They say that I'm royalty too, that I was snatched away from the palace in London by them and given to my parents to look after because the servants at the palace were cruel to me. So you see really I'm a princess."

She paused for effect.

"If you're a princess then why have you got cross eyes." asked the little girl.

"It's the reason that the servants were cruel to me," said Emily, wiping an imaginary tear from the corner of her eye. The fairies said it shows I have magic and the servants didn't like it – they'd have killed me probably if the fairies hadn't rescued me. So I don't mind living amongst common people, but one day I will have to go back to London and be a queen."

"What do the fairies look like?"

"Oh, they're beautiful. They have beautiful robes and the royal ones have tiny gold crowns with tiny jewels in them, and they have pretty little wings and can fly as fast as a bird, and they land on my hand when I hold it out."

She held a hand out and all the smaller girls stared at it, but no fairies appeared.

"Have you got a crown?" one of the girls asked.

"She's never seen a fairy. She makes it up that's why she's got no friends!" That was Billy who'd stopped counting and decided to put Emily straight on a few things.

"Well I wouldn't want friends like you William Richmond! The fairies are all the friends I need."

The little girls were distracted by something and used Billy's interruption as a cover they wandered off leaving the two older kids bickering.

"I've seen a fairy and it's nothing like what you say Emily, you just make up stories!"

"You're a fibber Billy!" Emily squealed in high indignation.

"Really?", he smirked. "Come with me tonight and maybe I'll show you a fairy for real."

"I'm not stupid, it's a trick! You don't know anything about fairies!", Emily was furious.

Billy put his hand in his pocket and drew out a small piece of green material about two and a half inches square. He held it up triumphantly betwixt finger and thumb, and smirked.

"What's that supposed to be?" Emily fumed.

"I pulled it off a fairy's coat." said Billy.

"Fibber!"

"Oh, well if that's what you think then you won't want to see it will you? And you'll never know." He went to stuff it back in his pocket.

"Wait!" Emily was uncertain. It seemed highly unlikely that Billy could have met a fairy, let alone acquired a piece of fairy clothing. And yet... so tantalizing.

"Let me see it please Billy." she wheedled.

Billy held it out, keeping a firm hold on it and allowed Emily to examine it.

It looked at first like a piece of grubby green cloth, but looked at closely the weave seemed almost none existent. It was fine like silk but much thicker, and if you held it close to your eyes then there was an unidentifiable goldish tinge to it when turned in the light. Emily had never seen cloth like it, nor had she felt anything like it, it was warm to the touch. She bent to sniff it.

"Don't wipe your nose on it!" said Billy disgustedly, "Use your cuffs like everyone else!"

"Us ladies have handkerchiefs, not like common people from the workhouse like you Billy."

"I am NOT from the workhouse and you know it!"

"Bet you end up there. Either that or on the end of a good piece of hemp rope."

Billy was impressed by her level of sarcastic ability and somewhat lost for words he allowed her to sniff the cloth. Something he'd not thought to even consider doing.

Emily's nostrils caught the briefest shade of an alien scent. Musty and intoxicating. In that moment she knew that what ever the cloth was she need to have it.

"Please William, may I have this? Please? I'll give you a kiss on the cheek."

Billy burst out laughing and snatched the cloth back, shoving it out of sight in his trouser pocket.

"Why would I want a kiss off an ugly, squit-eyed cow like you

Emily?" He guffawed

Emily's face dropped, her bottom lip trembled, and her cheeks reddened with embarrassment. She looked down to hide her eyes from him, so that he could not see her squint. A tear rolled down her left cheek and dropped off, falling through the air before splashing onto the floor. It was quickly followed by one from her right eye. She snuffled, trying not to let Billy see her crying, but the dam had been breached and the tears would not stop. She started to sob under her breath.

Billy felt awful. He knew not to tease someone about their deformities – at least not to their face and he had spoken in haste, and in anger, she had called him a liar after all. He thought about the patch – it wasn't something he particularly wanted to keep, he had no need of a keepsake for that little green monster. He pulled it out of his pocket and offered it. Emily had started to make a high pitched whining noise to accompany the tears which was growing steadily in volume.

"Emily."

She noticed what was hanging from his fingers.

"I, I was wrong to say that. You're not ugly, nor a cow. Honestly."

"I am squit-eyed though aren't I?"

There was no denying it. Billy squirmed inwardly. "It doesn't matter. No-one's perfect are they? Two of Jonathan's toes are webbed?"

"What!? Like a frog? That's, that's....... horrid!"

"Shhhh. You mustn't tell anyone. Here take the cloth, you can have it."

"Oh William! Thank you."

"You don't have to kiss me. I'm giving I to you for free."

He really didn't want to be kissed by Emily, he'd never live it down if anyone saw it.

Too late! She leaned forward and kissed him on the cheek. Billy blushed and prayed that no-one had seen it happen.

Emily was engrossed with the cloth, now easily convinced that Billy was telling the truth this small patch had become her greatest treasure. She noticed the small hole where the tip of Billy's knife had pierced the cloth.

"There's a hole in it." she observed.

Yes I caught it with my knife.

She gasped. "William! Did you stab a fairy?" she was aghast.

"No, it's not what you think Emily. It wasn't a good fairy at all. It tried to drag me off."

"To fairyland?"

"I don't know, I guess, maybe. It was down a dark tunnel. I don't think it was a place you'd want to visit."

"Billy, you must tell me where the tunnel to fairyland is. I must see it."

Billy hesitated and was saved by the hand bell being rung by Mr

Hawkins which denoted that lunch time was over. He ran off to his class, leaving a happy Emily trailing in his wake wiping the tears off her face with her cuffs.

Chapter 16 - The retreat from Mons – the find

As Bill was looking down from the cart at the body of the dead fairy he became gradually aware of a whistling noise that increased in intensity. He knew he should dive off the wagon and take cover but his leg was screaming at him not to – the shell might miss and he might not get hurt, on the other hand if he jumped he wouldn't miss the ground and hurting was a certainty.
"Whizz-bang!" shouted the driver using the slang term for an incoming shell.
He gave Bill a mighty shove that propelled him off the seat and towards the waiting and painful looking ground, he threw himself the other way. Bill yelled and squirmed in the air trying to pick a landing position which would give the least grief to his leg. By and large he succeeded, landing on his other leg, so he was jarred but there was no direct blow to his wound. He just had time to register his own impact when the shell followed suit. It actually landed harmlessly in the field beside him and failed to detonate. It would be dug up by a farmer ploughing his land eighty years later. He placed it in the gateway of the field with several other items of munitions. Later it was collected by and army unit who transported it to a safe area and finally detonated it safely.

Bill opened his eyes after a few seconds of not hearing an explosion, and registered the dead gaze of the fairy lying a couple of feet in front of him. Ignoring the aching in his leg he reached forward and undid the belt on it's tunic. He slid off the knife in its sheath and the small pouch, which seemed to be made of greenish leather.

He unbuttoned his uniform tunic and slipped the items inside, and rebuttoned the tunic with it's brass buttons. The professional soldier in him protested at the dullness of the brass, which, like his boots buckle and cap badge, had not been polished since before his unit mobilised to go to France. Smart and shiny might be nice in peacetime but glinting metal in wartime might just attract a bullet and was therefore prohibited. As he got to his knees the cart driver reached him and with as much care as could be mustered helped him back to his feet and then climbed back up in order to pull Bill back up to his seat.

"That was a close call." said the driver after a long pause. Bill looked at him, he was ashen under his peaked cap, his hands on the reigns were trembling. "Sorry I pushed you off."

"If that one had been a live one then you could have saved my life back there." Said Bill, attempting humour and trying to smile through the throbbing pain at the same time.

"Next time." said the driver and laughed nervously.

That evening the wounded were lodged in a cluster of barns on a Belgium farm. Exhausted, Bill lay on a pile of straw for a bed. It was hardly ideal for the wounded but the nurses and medical staff were running around making the very best of the facilities that they had, in this they were aided by a group of Belgium nuns who bustled around fetching and carrying and saying soothing words to the patients. Sadly most of them only spoke French and most of the troops being British only spoke English. The lone wounded Belgian soldier identifiable by his dark blue coat and grey blue trousers, who had pitched up in the barn for some reason, did speak English and probably spoke French too, but it seemed that he was from the Dutch speaking part of Belgium and much preferred to speak English than French to which he had an aversion and would only speak to the nuns if he had too.

Bill's leg was throbbing again despite the attention of the nurses. He lay on his side facing the wall so that he wasn't putting any weight on his bad leg and remembered the fairy from earlier. He unbuttoned his tunic and reached inside pulling out the knife and the pouch which he opened. Inside were worms, maggots, beetles and caterpillars which writhed and made a bid for freedom at the sight of light. Revolted he threw the thing from him. It landed in a pile of straw and disappeared into it. Well, at least he now knew what fairies ate! At least he presumed he did. He pulled the knife from it's scabbard and examined it. The handle was different from what he remembered of the one he had seen as a child. That one had a single green stone. This appeared to have a series of smaller green and clear stones set roughly around the edge of the pommel. The handle seemed to be made of stags antler, although of a greenish hue. The blade seemed to be copper, and was dull in colour apart from the edge which gleamed. He stroked his thumb across the blade and noted that despite it's looks it was as keen as a razor. He stroked it across the stubble on his face and winced, it was sharp enough to shave but he really needed some soap to pull it off properly. Instead he picked up a stalk of straw and proceeded to split it multiple times into ever finer strips. When he became bored of this he put the knife away in its scabbard and placed it back inside his tunic. Carefully, to avoid straining his leg, he rolled onto his back and thought back to his childhood. The sight of the fairy had awoken some very unwelcome memories.

Chapter 17 - After school.

Dodging Emily at the end of lunch time turned out to be just a temporary reprieve, she was waiting for him at the end of the day and promptly cornered him as he went to investigate the new gate by the toilet block.

"William, you must tell me where the fairies live. No! You must show me instead, take me there now. Please, please, PLEASE?"

He looked around wildly for his mates, but they had filed out of the gate and had turned left up the street. The park was to the right, so he wasn't sure where they were going. He wasn't sure whether the fact that they hadn't noticed was good or bad. If they had been there it was debatable whether they would have helped free him from Emily's attentions or would just have used it as an excuse to taunt him. On balance probably the later.

"I'm not telling you or taking you." he hissed, "I'll tell you about it, but don't ask me about where it was, it's dangerous. I think he snatches children."

"Fairies don't do that! They're good and kind!"

"I know what I saw and I know what happened. Look would you let me walk you home and I'll tell you, but not if you keep interrupting."

"Oh, William! You never would?"

"I said I would, and stop calling me William. Only my mom and the wicked witch call me that. It's Billy."

"There's a witch? Oh wait, you mean Miss. Ball don't you?"

"I never said that." said Billy starting to panic. The last thing he wanted in the current situation was for Emily to blab it out that he had called Miss Ball a witch. People might wonder what else he did behind Miss. Ball's back – literally, "Come on."

They walked slowly, Billy wondering what idiotic notion had made him agree to walk with Emily, if he was seen he'd never be allowed to forget it and the rest of his life at school would be a misery.

"Well, I was playing in.. well somewhere, and I was sat minding my own business, on my own and while I was hiding.."

"Why were you hiding?"

"I just was."

"Who were you hiding from Billy?"

"No one, I was just hiding, practising hiding. It's something we boys do."

"Were you hiding from the policeman?"

"No, I want to be a soldier. Sometimes you have to be able to hide to spot the enemy, that's why they wear khaki uniforms, so they can hide better."

"What's khaki?"

"It's a colour, sort of brown, but lighter, it's so you can hide better."

"Well the soldiers at Buckingham Palace wear red."

"That's different. They aren't hiding are they?"

"Well no, but if your in the countryside it's green isn't it? What good is ...kacky? Karty? Ka.."

"Khaki. It's khaki. Kar – kar as in car-nival, key as in door key, but I think it's spelt different. And yes it's green in England, but the rest of the Empire isn't is it? A lot of it's like, dusty and sandy so it sort of blends in well – like South Africa last year with the Boers. South Africa's dusty. Everyone thinks it's jungle because it's Africa but Mr Jones down our road was there at the Battle of Rorkes Drift when the Zulus were there. He says it's all dusty and it's really hard for stuff to grow. Sometimes he still thinks the Zulus are after him and he shouts and yells, and Mrs. Jones has to calm him down and get him back into the house. Mom says he should really be in the asylum but Mrs. Jones won't hear of it. Anyway, most of the empire is dusty coloured so khaki is good."

"Canada isn't dusty. It's trees and snow."

"No but there isn't any enemy in Canada, that's why Mounties wear red, they'll all Canadians, apart for the Eskimos in the snowy bit and they don't hurt anyone, they just catch fish through holes in the ice."

Emily got bored of this game and decided to get back to the fairy.

"I thought you was going to tell me about the fairy. You were hiding?"

"Yes, I was hiding and.."

"From nothing."

"I wasn't hiding from nothing! Sam was.. - Emily!! You trickster! I'm not telling you where it was so forget it. Do you want to hear the rest or not?

"Yes please Billy, you're good at telling this story."

"No more tricks?"

Emily put on her most believable, honest and angelic face and shook her head. Billy tried not to laugh as her eyes went all over the place. He was starting to like this strange girl, only a bit mind, and not in any mushy lovie way. It was a shame she wasn't a lad because he thought she'd make a jolly good pal since she was obviously clever and chatty and seemed to know stuff, and she'd seen something he's only seen pictures of - the Guards in London. This was Billy's dream – to be a Guardsman in the Grenadier Guards and wear a red tunic and black bearskin. He just prayed that when he grew up he would be over six foot – the height requirement for the four Guards regiments. So far he was a long way off, but there was time.

They smiled at each other and Billy told her the story of how the fairy had been observed, how it had opened the hawthorn patch, but the fairy's knife became a sword and thus the final fight between the two of them became a little more heroic and impressive. Emily listened and was more or less silent as she absorbed ever tiniest morsel of information. Any trace of disbelief was gone and by the time he came to the bit about being trapped and immobilised by the hawthorn she was in awe of Billy.

"How ever did you get out?" she asked breathlessly.

"Well, fortunately for me some of my friends happened to be going past and I shouted to them and they came and pulled the branches away from me and got me out."

"Do they know how you was trapped?" She asked.

"No, do you think a boy would ever believe me about seeing a fairy? They'd never let me live it down? They'd tease me the same way we tease..." he stopped short uncertain how to proceed.

"The same way you tease me?" she finished the sentence for him.

Billy blushed deeply. "I guess we do, don't we." Emily said nothing, so Billy ploughed on, "I've been horrible to you Emily. It won't happen again – not from me because now I know you I think you are a really nice person, you're a bit funny, but your not a loony like I thought."

She giggled and then laughed, and then looking both ways up and down the street to make sure no one was watching she kissed him on the cheek – for the second time. Billy was mortified, but also at the same time a little bit thrilled, and he felt himself blush again.

When they arrived at Emily's house he said to her, "Emily, you won't tell anyone what I said will you? It has to be our secret."

"Everyone thinks I make things up anyway, so even if I did tell them they'd likely not believe me, but no I promise I won't tell."

"Promise me something else too?"

"What do you want me to promise?"

"You must not go looking for the fairy. It was evil Emily, it tried to kidnap me and if I hadn't had my knife with me it would have dragged me off to goodness knows where. And I don't think I was the first one."

Emily went wide eyed as well as cross eyed. "What do you mean Billy?"

"Well George's grandma, Mrs. Hope? Well she said when she was a little girl another girl went missing, she was last seen in the.. in the same place that I saw the fairy and they never found her, but they did find a little boy's skeleton who had gone missing fifty years or so before, again in the very same place. He's got a plaque in the church by the font."

"How did they know it was him?"

"He had buttons, silver ones, he was a nob," said Billy using the nick name for nobility, "and had a horse and everything, a racing horse mind not a nag like the milkman uses, which came back on it's own without him and when they searched for this girl that Mrs. Hope knew that's when they found his buttons with his skeleton, that's how they knew it was him."

"Gosh!" said Emily, "I rather like the milkman's horse, she's called Copenhagen. Because the milkman's dad's, dad's, dad, I think, fought at a battle with a famous general and his horse was called Copenhagen, so that's why he called it that."

"Which battle and which general?"

"How should I know? Us ladies aren't interested in old battles and stuffy old generals what are probably dead by now anyway, nor soldiers unless they are handsome and brave and looking for a good wife, but I do like horses. I shall own one one day and ride it side saddle too."

"Yes, the milkman's horse isn't a bad horse, and I quite like it – I even gave it an apple core once, but it's not the sort of horse you'd ride if you was a nob is it?"

"I think you'd make a handsome soldier Billy. You'd look good as a soldier in a red jacket outside the palace; not in kar-key though, you're too handsome for that."

Blushing, was rapidly becoming quite a habit for young Billy.

The next day Emily made a detour on the way home, Billy had gone off with his mates. She went to the church, walked up the path and opened the door which was always open during the day, and went and sat near the front in the pews, from where she could see quite a few plaques and monuments on the wall. It didn't take long to find the one dedicated to Robert Neville. 1802 – she did some mental arithmetic – ninety eight years ago. Emily's favourite subject at school was arithmatic, she always did well in tests and had a fondness for numbers. For want of anything else to do she played with the number in her head. Half of ninety eight was forty nine which was seven times seven, which meant that ninety eight was fourteen times seven or two lots of seven times seven. Seven was Emily's favourite and indeed lucky number. She believed it was magic and seven times seven must be very magic. She looked again at the plaque and wondered what Robert Neville had been like. Rich? Well, yes if he was a nob and rode a race horse like Billy said. Handsome? She thought so. She thought it might be nice to say a prayer for his soul, so she pulled out a hassock, the kneeling cushion, out of the pew in front of her, put it on the floor and knelt on it. Once she was comfortable she put her hands together, closed her eyes and prayed.

"Lord I pray Lord that you will look after Robert Neville for ever Lord, in Heaven Lord and I hope that when his horse died it went to heaven too Lord, and that he is riding it in Heaven Lord and that he won't fall off and if he does Lord that you will catch him in your arms Lord. Amen."

"Amen."

She opened her eyes and whipped round. The vicar was stood at the back of the church. He'd been in the vestry at his desk writing correspondence and had heard the little footsteps enter the church and had stepped around the vestry door next to the entrance just to check it someone had come to make mischief; several of the oak pews had initials carved in them. Initials of which the last letter always seemed to be 'S'. He couldn't prove it but he strongly suspected some of the members of the Steptoe clan.

"That was a lovely prayer Emily" he said, "Would you mind if I join you?"

"Of course Reverend, it's your church after all."

"Well, actually more properly it's God's church. I just look after it for him, or his people anyway." The vicar looked up at the plaque and frowned. "I'm curious, Emily, why were you praying for Robert Neville in particular?"

"Well, I heard he disappeared while he was out on his horse and they found his bones and buttons years and years later when they were looking for a little girl."

"Ah yes, that would be little Enid."

"Did they find her eventually?"

The vicar smiled, despite the pain he felt inside. A pain from, he counted quickly, forty nine years ago. The first child's funeral he'd conducted after moving to Bartholomew's – albeit a funeral without a body. He sat down on the pew in front of Emily and swivelled round so he could talk to her.

"No," he said, "We never found her God rest her soul."

"Where did they find Robert's body? And why didn't they find it before?" Emily asked.

"Hmm? Oh, it was hidden in a patch of brambles.. no I tell a lie it was hawthorns. A big patch. I would think the poor little chap was thrown from his horse and landed in the bush. He must've hit his head and fractured his skull or broken his neck and lain there for forty nine years, until they were looking for Enid. The plaque came from the old church before this one, but his grave is outside if you want to see it. It's about twenty yards off the path on the right hand side as you go out. You can't miss it, there's an angel kneeling on it praying."

"Oh, I know the one. She's called Mildred?"

"Is she?"

"Yes."

"Sorry, who is called Mildred?"

"The angel of course Reverend."

"Oh." the vicar had had conversations with Emily before and was used to the sudden turns and flights of fantasy which her thought processes took."

"I didn't know that Emily. Did she tell you that herself?"

Emily looked him up and down slowly, which was disconcerting because he wasn't sure which eye she was using, and then started to shake her head slowly. "No... she's made of stone, she can't talk. I gave her the name. She's not real you know."

"Ah.", said the vicar chuckling to himself.

Emily grinned. "So, where were was the hawthorn bush?"

The vicar knew exactly where wasop the hawthorn bush was, but there seemed something strange about Emily's light hearted morbidness that unsettled him slightly. He felt guided not to tell her where the hawthorn bush was. "Oh, it was on the heath. The heath has long gone."

Emily looked doubtful, Billy had been told to stay away from the place where the bones were found, the same place he'd seen the fairy in the hawthorn bush, so it still existed, but at the same time it didn't seem right that a vicar could tell fibs. Now Billy, that was a different story. She'd have to think about that. In fact the vicar hadn't 'fibbed' at all. He hadn't said anything about the hawthorn bush not being there, just that the heath was gone. He merely neglected to mention that it had been tamed and used as the park. Well most of it had been tamed.

"I have to go go now Reverend." Emily said.

"Yes, you get off and thank you for the chat Emily. Take care, God bless and I'll see you on Sunday."

She smiled. "Bye bye Reverend", then she got up and went to the door, exited the church and skipped down the path greeting Mildred the angel on the way. Mildred stayed silent, she was after all made of stone.

The next day Emily took a different tack. After class she walked to Mr. Hawkins class room. She knocked and when she heard Mr Hawkins intone the word "Come." she entered and then walked up to Mr. Hawkins' desk and stood there waiting politely to be noticed.

She liked Mr. Hawkins, he was a kindly gentleman and she, like the rest of her class, was hoping that they could have him in replacement for Miss Ball. Mr Hawkins kept reading the book he had in front of him, in truth he was playing for time while he remembered Emily's name; she was new to him and things like learning children's names took time these days, but what he lacked in sharpness he more than made up for in wisdom and he knew it would come.

Emily grew impatient and started to open her mouth. Without looking up from his book Mr Hawkins slowly raised one forefinger to signal her not to talk. After a few more moments he snapped the book shut and beamed at the little cross-eyed girl before him. "Yes Emily?"

"Mr. Hawkins, did you know we used to have a heath?"

"Why yes, we did.", He fumbled in his jacket pocket under his black robe and produced his pipe and tobacco. Emily watched fascinated as he opened his battered tobacco tin, pulled out a large pinch of tobacco and pushed it down into the bowl of the pipe with his finger. He talked as he worked. "We don't have one now though. Do you know what happened to it?"

"No Mr. Hawkins, I was hoping you could tell me where it went."

"Ah well, it's still where it was. It's just been tidied and renamed."

Emily looked puzzled.

"For the Queen's jubilee, not this last one, the one before, the Golden one, it became the Jubilee Park."

"Ohhhh! Thank you Mr Hawkins. Do you know if any hawthorns grow there?"

"I don't know Emily. It's been years since I went down there. You'll have to check yourself I'm afraid."

"Thank you Mr. Hawkins. May I go now please?"

"Of course you may." And with those words Emily's fate was sealed.

Chapter 18 - Emily meets the fairy.

There were several hawthorn bushes and hedges in and around the park. Ornamental ones which were clipped and trimmed, and there were others in the hedge which bounded the park on two sides where there was no fence. Emily looked at them all in turn, and finally wound up standing in the corner by the large clump between the oak and the ash trees. The wind was starting to lift and the trees were rustling their leaves like the roaring of an angry sea. Overhead the clouds were turning grey and drifting in – they promised rain. Emily put her hand into her pocket and found the silky patch of fairy cloth, she pulled it out and held it looking at it and feeling it's odd texture. She looked around and saw a few people in the park. There were an elderly couple sitting on a bench in the ornamental garden area of the park. As normal there were kids playing on the swings on the other side of the park, where one day a decent collection of sturdy playthings would join them. She concluded that no one was close enough to notice or disturb her. A sudden gust of wind snatched the fairy cloth from her hand and blew it upwards.

"No!" she squealed. "No, come back!"

The wind dropped momentarily and so did the cloth then as she grabbed for it, it flipped in mid air and went straight into hawthorn bush a few feet in front of her. Emily, thankful, dashed up. She could see the cloth which was sitting about six inches inside the thorns and easily reachable but something strange was happening. The bush seemed to be almost melting very slowly before her eyes around the cloth. Puzzled she stood still and watched, trying to make sense of what her eyes were seeing. The wind didn't help, making the fine branches and their leaves wave back and forward. She realised that the cloth was somehow working it's way further into the bush, but that didn't really make any sense, it was like the thorns were retreating and dragging the cloth with it. She wasn't going to put her hand in there because it might snag her sleeves and ladies didn't do stuff like that. She looked around for a stick. She could see a suitable branch a few yards away and walked to fetch it. It wasn't long enough, so she looked further and found what she was looking for on the far side of the oak tree. Dropping the first stick , she picked up the second one, returned to the front of the hawthorns, and was shocked by what she found. There was a tunnel, low and dim, but with enough light to see clearly by. The entrance to fairyland stood before her, her heart was pounding fit to burst. Billy's warnings about fairies being evil were going through her head, but this was too exciting. There on the floor, which seemed to be made of old cobblestones with mossy gaps between them, was the patch of cloth. She hesitated, checking the inside of the tunnel which bent away to the right after a short distance, and then she stepped very softly inside. In four paces she reached the cloth and stooped down to reach it. As she extended her hand there was a sound of falling rain from behind her. She looked over her shoulder realising that the threatening clouds had burst and that in her rush to get to the park she had left her coat on the hook in the cloakroom adjoining her classroom. She would have to go back and get it or be in trouble when she got home, although she would get very wet on the way. She noticed the rather soothing and dreamy smell of the place, and breathed deeply. Her fingers closed on the cloth but as she pulled it something pulled gently from the other side. She snapped her head back and found herself looking into two gold eyes like sovereigns in a small green face, which belonged to a small green man. Wings were visible over his shoulders and he wore a green tunic with an area which was slightly darker than the rest of it obviously where the pocket had been pulled from by Billy. She gasped with shock.

"Don't be afraid." he whispered, gently lifting up the cloth which they both held in their finger tips. "You found my pocket! You brought it back. We will have to find a reward for you."

"A reward?"

She felt slightly woozy with the smell.

"Yes, you must come with me to get a reward." He smiled

Emily was suddenly unsure, something wasn't right. Billy had said he was green, but now she wondered why that should be. It seemed rude to mention that a persons colour wasn't what she expected, but again despite what Billy had said she was expecting something much smaller, so she said uncertainly, "Aren't you a little tall to be a fairy?"

"Yes." She loosed the cloth, stopped backwards and turned to leave. She was met with a solid wall of hawthorn. As quickly and quietly as it had opened the tunnel had closed behind her. She panicked and spun back to face the little green man, "I'm a goblin.". He was still smiling, but it had changed and there was nothing gentle about it any more. Emily screamed.

In the days that followed Emily's disappearance Mr Hawkins, the teacher, would be identified as the last person to see Emily alive, it was his recollection of this last conversation which led to a search of the park and the hawthorn bush where the searchers found no trace of Emily, but did discover the remains of poor little Enid, who had been missing for forty nine years and was at last laid to rest in the grave where her parents were buried. Her parents had been buried in a pauper's grave, there hadn't been money or a monument any more than there had been money for winter fuel. The headstone included their names, and the kindness of the parishioners in providing it, meant for the first time in a long time they too were properly remembered.

For the rest of his days Mr Hawkins was haunted by the thought that if he had said something different, Emily might not have vanished.

Chapter 19 - Bob Helen reminisces.

Bob sat back in his chair whilst Mrs. Helen rattled around in the kitchen preparing a late supper for him. He had offered to have a cold sandwich, but she was very old fashioned and supportive in her view that her husband provided for her and when he came home from work she provided for him. That meant he came home to a home where there wasn't a pin out of place and he came home to a proper cooked meal not a cold sandwich. Tonight it would be liver by the smell of it, probably with mashed potatoes, peas and onion gravy. He wasn't feeling too good, starting to sweat and feel a little feverish – the onset of a bout of malaria, contracted in Borneo during the war, when like an idiot, he'd chosen to be blasé about taking his medication. He really didn't need this while he was searching non stop for Daniel Smith. He could work through it, but he was painfully aware that it was going to make things harder for him. He got up from his chair and went to the sideboard, a long low piece of furniture against the wall opposite the fire and mantelpiece. He opened one of the doors and took out a glass and two bottles. From the green one he poured gin and after putting it away he poured tonic water from the clear bottle with the yellow label. He walked back to his chair swilling the two liquids together in the glass, then he sat down and sipped at his drink. The quinine in the tonic water would help the malaria, the gin would disguise the taste of the tonic water.

Gin and tonic had been invented for this very purpose. He clutched his glass in his right hand, rested his arm on the arm of the chair and let his head loll backwards. He thought back to the first episode of malaria he'd suffered. That had been bad. His group of Chindits, elite troops operating behind enemy lines were liasing with the local Jap hating natives and using their hill top village with it long-houses raised on stilts as a temporary base as they passed through. The natives, Kachin tribes-people, kept themselves to themselves for the most part, not even mixing with neighbouring villages much unless it was to take a head or two. You could tell who had taken heads because they had tattoos on their faces to prove it and small brass heads, or was it small brass skulls? He couldn't remember now, but anyway one brass head or skull for every head taken on a necklace. The heads were placed in one of the long house roofs or above the door, along with the heads of the ancestors – that made for a lot of heads. The Japanese invasion had provided them with a once in a lifetime opportunity. The Kachins had long ago come to an agreement with the ruling British. The British had left them alone for the most part, but did discourage the taking of heads and in return the Kachins got certain benefits; medicines, good quality metal goods and missionaries who had made some headway into converting the tribes to Christianity and moved them away from head hunting. The Japanese with their cruel treatment of the local peoples had not bargained with the savagery and jungle skills of a supposedly inferior native race armed with spears and machetes. The British had found them to be ready allies, and set to with a will, training them with modern weapons and receiving training in tracking, camouflage and survival in return, Head hunting was suddenly very much the vogue again amongst the Kachin warriors. Many of the heads that Bob had seen in their villages had a distinctive Japanese look to them.

When he had his first bout of malaria Bob was considered by the platoon medic to be that ill that was borderline to accompany them, likely to be a hindrance. He was given a colossal roasting for not taking his anti malaria pills, despite the fact that he lied and maintained that he had taken them, and then while the rest of the patrol that he was part of left their village base to bed down for the night with the column of over four hundred men camped around the area he was left in ignominy shaking and sweating in the village after being dosed up with quinine, which the medic personally watched him take. He had his rifle, a Mk.III version of the Lee Enfield that Bill Richmond would have been familiar with in the trenches, to get it he'd swapped the more modern No.4 rifle that he'd been issued with an Indian soldier because of the earlier rifle's longer bayonet and the mistaken belief that because it was hand instead of machine finished, it was therefore a better weapon – but mainly because of the bayonet; seventeen inches of cold steel instead of the miserable six inch prong that the No.4

came with. He spent some time cleaning the weapon, all the time surrounded by a little group of Kachin children who laughed and chattered at him. Once it was spotless he pulled out his khukri, the traditional weapon of the Gurkhas, but also used by the Chindits for its effectiveness as both a weapon and as a useful tool for clearing a path. In truth they tried to avoid hacking at the undergrowth, there was so much of it for a start, plus the fact that chopped plants gave a lovely trail to follow and the sound of chopping itself could alert the enemy to your presence. In an environment where men could stand ten yards apart and not see each other, moving quietly and very slowly was the order of the day. A five minute walk off the track could leave you lost forever, walking on the track might mean walking into an ambush. Everything in the jungle seemed to want to sting, bite, scratch or eat you. Wounds, especially from leeches would fester quickly if not cared for properly and yet there was a lot to like about the jungle. It was just that Bob couldn't think of anything to like at the moment. He checked the sharpness of the kukri. People would have you believe that a kukri, once drawn could not be re-sheathed until it had tasted blood. That was a myth, the amount of times that the Chindits and Gurkhas used their kukris every day would have meant death by blood loss. Once he was satisfied that the blade was sharp enough not to need sharpening he lay down and curled up on the floor on a bamboo mat which was actually filthy, but there were few other options and in the state he was currently he couldn't have cared less.

He woke suddenly, unaware that he'd drifted off. He was cold and shivering violently, yet knew he was burning up, and his head was pounding like someone was using a jack hammer on the inside of his skull. He felt sick, having already thrown up several times before the medic left him high and dry with a bunch of murderous head hunting maniacs, friendly murderous head hunting maniacs it had to be said, but still murderous head hunting maniacs. He reached for his water bottle, pulled out the cork on its string and took a good drink. Then he looked out of the doorway to see what the commotion was that had woken him.

Most of the village seemed to have gathered around something. They were angry and shouting. No one else was in the long house and no one was watching him. He rose unsteadily to his feet and shuffled to the door to get a better view. Something was screaming, it didn't sound human so it must be some kind of animal. He could see a bamboo cage, small and freshly made, it was being jostled and thumped. Whatever was inside was being poked with sticks. Someone pushed a spear with a knife blade secured to it's end through the bars. It wasn't a stab, just a poke but it produced an unearthly screech which scattered the natives back several yards and made Bob jump. Then, with the crowd dispersed for a few seconds he got a clear view of the monkey inside the cage – a green monkey? It swung around in it's cage and he saw two terrible long jagged wounds on its back, which seemed to be dripping green blood, and then it's two bright golden eyes and a set of sharp looking white teeth. The crowd closed in laughing and there was another screech as the makeshift spear was pushed between the bars. The crowd ran back again, still laughing, he saw that they were mainly women and children. One of the men turned and saw Bob standing by the door. Bob recognised him as one of those with a reasonable level of English, but couldn't remember his name. Some of the patrol had Christened him "Four heads", because of the four tattoos on his face and the little brass baubles around his neck, although there were several men with four tattoos, he was the only one of them who could speak English. He grinned at Bob and blew out smoke from a cigarette in his hand which he'd cadged form one of the troops.

"We call him Pan-kike Belu." he said,"You call him he who bites flowers.". He grinned again, obviously this explained everything. Bob remained unenlightened. The creature screeched again, Bob noticed that the person with the knife on the stick was a woman. Unlike the others she wasn't laughing, she was screaming with rage and tears flowed down her face. A small dirty, frightened looking child of indeterminate sex clutched the hand that wasn't holding the spear.

Four heads decided to try again "You not have Pan-kike Belu in

England?"

"I don't think so. What is it?"

"What is it? It is try steal woman child, she catch and punish it."

"Is it a monkey?" Bob was intrigued.

"Monkey? No, no monkey. I tell you is Pan-kike Belu." There was some shouting from the group, a strange high pitched voice which after a moment Bob realised was coming form the monkey – pankybeloo thing in the cage. "It can talk? Asked bob, his jaw dropping

"Yes, Pan-kike Belu talk to children so they can take children away."

"What... what's it saying now?"

"It wants let go. And knife it burns it. Not likening much."

"Will they kill it?"

Four heads laughed. "Not let this one go. Kill slow and throw body in river to take away – no good to eat. That way no take children away ever."

Bob felt sick again and vomited out of the doorway narrowly missing four heads, who didn't seem that bothered. There was a grunting from under the hut and a large greyish pig appeared from between the stilts on which the long house was built and to which it had been tethered and proceeded to clean up the unexpected bonus in short order. Bob looked at it and felt faint. His head was worse than ever and he needed to lie down. He staggered back to his makeshift bed and dropped down so he could die (hopefully) and instead passed out and slept.

When he next woke it was morning. The medic was back with a couple of other soldiers and the native Kachins and they were enjoying a meal – the British out of mess tins and the Natives off banana leaves. Tom, the medic saw him sitting up and came over.
"How's it going?" Tom asked.
"Well I still feel rough but resting over night helped"
"Over night? You've missed an entire day. Fortunately for you it was a rest day otherwise we'd have had to leave you?" laughed Tom. "Four heads and his wife have been looking after you. Take this." He gave Bob some more quinine and again watched him swallow it. "He says you've been delirious, and he thought you might die. Your lucky we didn't come back and find you grinning down at us from the rafters." he gestured upwards.
Bob looked up and saw the shrivelled, blackened heads looking down with empty eye sockets at him. "Very funny!" he said without a trace of humour.
Tom laughed, "Feeling any better?"
"A bit." Bob had a weird memory of a cage with something in it.
"Fancy some grub?"
"What is it?"
"Rice with pork."
"Oh no..." The vague image of the Pan-kike Belu was replaced with the vivid recollection of the pig snuffling up a pool of vomit,

his vomit. And his stomach turned. It was probably the very same pig which is why it was tethered beneath the hut.

Four heads looked across from the group. "Hey! You awake, good you not die. You feed pig, pig feed us. Good yes? Ha, ha, ha!"

Bob didn't say anything. Tom nudged him and whispered, "Between you and me I think he's a little disappointed you didn't die on him." He grinned and drew his finger across his throat whilst rolling his eyes upwards.

Bob jerked back to wakefulness nearly spilling his gin and tonic in the process. He sat upright, sweating still, but with a thought in his head which disturbed him greatly.

Normally Bob and his wife didn't really talk about his work at home, he didn't believe it was right to bring his work home with him to burden her with. Instead they chatted about day to day life, they played cards, or listened to the radio or gramophone together and Mrs. Helen was a pretty good pianist, so they weren't short of things to do together, but tonight was one of those which broke the rule. Mrs. Helen and Mrs. Smith knew each other and it was therefore a personal matter when it came to Daniel's safety, in fact a large proportion of the town's population were now aware and concerned. Over dinner they chatted.

"Any news on little Daniel?" she asked.

"No, I'm afraid not love. We've looked everywhere and spoken to everyone we can think of. Division will be bussing some PC's in tomorrow to really start with door to doors and start searching in earnest."

"Do you think..." she left the sentence unfinished, but her damp eyes betrayed her thoughts.

"I don't know what to think. I've never dealt with this kind of thing before. Missing kids yes, but they're always round at a friends or got lost, or forgotten the time. Sometimes they do run away and they turn up at a railway station without a ticket in a big city somewhere – I'm hoping that's what Daniel's done, but there were no sightings at the railway station. The last sighting was by his sister in Hob's Lane by the park, I picked his tracks up on the other side of the fence and we found his school cap, but after that the tracks stopped and there was nothing else there. It's like something just snatched him away."

"Something?"

"Hmmm?"

"You said 'something' Bob, 'something snatched him away', surely you mean someone."

Bob looked slightly perturbed, "Yes, of course." He took his handkerchief from his pocket and wiped his sweaty brow.

His wife reached across and touched the back of his free hand. He turned it and took her hand softly and squeezed it gently.

"I think I need to make a phone call, and then get back out there

I'm afraid."

"I understand dear." She smiled, "That poor little lad, I know if anyone can find him you can."

In the hall with the door closed Bob picked up the heavy Bakelite phone and rang the operator. He asked to be put through to Bill Richmond's number. Bill picked up the receiver within a few rings.

"Sergeant, it's Bob Helen. You know that chat we had about angels and erm, fairies?"

There was a stony silence for several seconds. "Go on." the reply eventually came in a voice which managed to convey that if he was taking the mick Bob would regret it.

He pressed on. "Did you see that picture in Daniel's notepad? The other night."

"The Green fairy in the Hawthorn bush?"

"Ye-es, that's the one. Well, I'm suffering with my malaria at the moment so if I sound like I've lost my mind blame it on that, okay?"

"Okay."

"Well, in Burma, I saw something, it's a bit tenuous, well very tenuous. The natives we were fighting alongside they captured a creature they said snatched children away, and they had it in a cage, they were going to kill it."

"What sort of creature, a big cat or something?"

"No, I thought it was a monkey at first, but it was green with gold eyes."

"I see where you're going with this Bob, did it have wings like the one in the picture by any chance?" To Bob's surprise there was no sense of disbelief, or mockery in the sergeant's voice. He wasn't sure if that was good or bad.

"No Sergeant, but it had two gouged wounds on its back, I think they may have ripped its wings off before I saw it. They were busy torturing it and it was speaking to them."

"It spoke? What did it say?"

"I don't know Sergeant, it was speaking in their language, Kachin. No wait, Four heads – our translator he told me erm... it begged to be released and said that a knife they were poking it with was burning it."

There was a clunk from the other end of the line.

"Sergeant? Are you there?"

There was a short pause and the Bill Richmond came back on the line.

"Sorry Bob, I dropped the receiver. This knife. Was it steel?"

"Err, yes, I guess so. I can't think of what else it could have been made of."

"Okay, that helps."

"It does?"

"Yes. Really. I'll explain later, but it does. Is there anything else you remember?"

"I don't think so, I'm lucky to remember that much, I was badly delirious with my first bout of malaria at the time."

"How bad is your malaria this time?"

"I'll live. Very sweaty, and a slight head ache but I'm fit for duty."

"Good. You were a Chindit? Did you have a machete for the jungle?"

"A kukri Sergeant"

"Even better. Still got it by any chance?"

"Yes Sergeant."

"Can you put your hand on it?"

Bob Helen glanced up at the wall above the telephone table where his kukri hung in its scabbard.

"Oh, yes."

"Good, get hold of it, and make sure it's sharp, where we're going I suspect that we might near to clear a bit of vegetation. I'll be round your house to pick you up in an hour , maybe two. I'll phone before I leave."

The sergeant was thinking of the time, as a boy, when he was trapped in the hawthorn patch. A sheath knife hadn't been much good then, but a kukri should do the job nicely if it came to it. Without saying another word he put the phone down.

Bob Helen put the receiver back on its cradle and reached up to take the kukri from it's nail in the wall. The leather sheath was dusty on the reverse from where it hadn't been disturbed for several years. Mrs Helen dusted it, but it wasn't something she'd want to take down off the wall. He pulled out his handkerchief, which was damp from mopping his brow, from his pocket and wiped it superficially clean. Then he drew the curved crescent blade from the scabbard and examined it. The back of the blade was thick tapering to a fine edge along the inner curve. Next to the handle was the funny little groove with a small post in the middle that meant that it looked like the foresight on a rifle. He wondered what it was really for. There were plenty of explanations; it was a Hindu fertility symbol, it was the image of a cow's hoof print – again sacred to the Hindu's, it was to trap an enemy's blade and break it, or to stop his blood flowing down the blade and making the handle slippery, it was also a sight for when you threw the thing – possibly like a boomerang. He grinned to himself and thought that most of those were unlikely, and doubted anyone really knew any more. He hefted it in his hand and felt it's familiar weight after all these years. Not a light weight weapon, or tool, depending on how you used it was none the less well balanced and the way that the blade widened before coming back in to a point meant that the weight was distributed in such a way as to make a chop very powerful. Between the broad part and the handle the blade was concave rather than convex which made it good for drawing along a branch or stick to produce fine shavings for starting a fire or shaping the stick with a degree of precision.

He drew his thumb across the blade with it's dull gleam and registered that it could indeed do with sharpening. With it in hand he walked through the house, much to the surprise of Mrs. Helen who asked "Where are you going with that old thing?" as he passed through the lounge.

"Chopping vegetation apparently, according to Sergeant Richmond." He grinned, "I'm going to sharpen it if I can find my stone in the shed."

"Chopping vegetation at this time of night?" She asked. "Well, you can chop the carrots for tomorrow night if you like." she quipped.

He laughed at the thought, and having located the household torch in the kitchen drawer he stepped out of the back door into the garden. He walked down the path and tested the torch as he went. A little dim but the batteries should be okay for the purpose. Unlike his police torch it was a cylinder type with a slide switch. He opened the door of his tool shed and stepped inside. Shining the torch around he quickly located the oil stone and the bottle shaped aluminium oil can with it's long curved copper pipe spout and trigger like pump handle on it's side. Negotiating the push powered lawn mower without catching his shins on it he put the kukri and torch on the small bench under the window and grabbed both the stone and oil bottle. He squirted some oil onto the stone, a slightly abrasive thing shaped a bit like an under devoped corn cob, and then set too with gentle precise stokes. Turning the kukri from time to time but always maintaining a correct angle between the stone and the blade edge. It was complex because the chopping edge had to be a coarser angle that the shaving edge and the tip, which was suitable for fine slicing, had to be even finer than the shaving edge. Three different edges on a twelve inch blade. "Like riding a bike." he said as he held it up in the torchlight after he was satisfied of it's sharpness, "You never forget."

He noticed a nick in the blade which he'd felt whilst sharpening, and another memory came back. A day in the jungle when a Japanese soldier screaming "Banzai!" rushed at him with a long fixed bayonet on his Arisaka rifle in the middle of a fire fight. Bob was halfway through reloading his rifle having fired all ten rounds. He had not yet fixed his bayonet. The bolt was open, and his hand was reaching towards the ammunition pouch on his chest for another clip of ammunition when he made eye contact with the Jap coming at him with wide, bloodshot eyes and flared nostrils. If he hadn't been screaming the Japanese battle cry then Bob might not have noticed him until it was too late. As it was, with about a second's notice, he threw his rifle forward at the enemy's legs with his left hand and at the same time his right hand forgot about the clip and instead swept backwards to his right hip and closed on the wooden handle of the kukri. It slid out of the scabbard as Bob turned his body to the right and stepped back allowing the bayonet and its accompanying rifle to slide harmlessly past, the Japanese soldier eyes registered a slight panic, Bob was swinging the kukri underhand along the underside of the rifle's fore-stock, it bit deep into the wood, freeing a gigantic splinter before connecting with one of the steel bands which held the top and bottom wood together, jarring both soldiers and putting the nick in the blade. This stopped the blade from slicing off the Jap's fingers which were curled tight just behind steel band. The Jap's legs caught Bob's thrown rifle and he tripped and fell forward, Bob pulled his arm back, brought the khukri forward before reversing the blow and swinging hard backwards. The blade hit the rear of the base of the enemy soldier's skull, just under the back of his helmet with it's net and its attendant camouflage foliage pushed through to make it hard to spot it's wearer. There was a sickening crunch and the cracking of bone. A fine spray of blood and tiny bone fragments flew from a large wound. Bob felt the blade stick fast and let go of the handle of his kukri leaving it embedded in the skull. The Japanese soldier stopped screaming his war cry instantly and crashed to the floor without making another sound. Bob didn't check to see if his opponent was dead or wounded, although he doubted the latter. He picked up his rifle, reloaded it with two clips of five .303" rounds, slammed the bolt closed, and continued the battle. He saw a movement to his left and instinctively ducked, and then threw himself flat as he saw what was coming. The blade of a samurai sword swept through the air and took his broad brimmed slouch hat with it as it connected near the top. Bob rolled and bought his rifle up fired, and missed. He yelped in terror and ripped the bolt back ejecting the spent round, before ramming it forward again and chambering another round. The sword had reached the apogee of it's arc and it's weilder, a ferocious looking Japanese officer, with a darker uniform than his troops, and a white shirt which had probably been crisp and fresh this morning but was now sweat soaked and a little grubby. The rifle roared again and Bob thought he'd missed again, but there was a small hole in the officer's tunic, on his right breast. He wavered slightly looking puzzled. In fact the powerful .303" bullet had passed straight through him and the wound it left on it"s exit was far more terrible than it's entry. Adrenalin kick in and the knuckles on his right hand tightened on the sword hilt. He brought his left had up to join the right and the sword continued to move downwards towards Bill. Bill had not paused and had again chambered another round, his hand dropped form the closed bolt and wrapped around the stock, his index finger tightened on the trigger. He yanked on the trigger, knowing that really a trigger should be squeezed to ensure accuracy, however there was no time for the niceties of target shooting, and once more the rifle jerked in his hands. This time the bullet tore into the officer's breast bone shattering it and causing mortal damage to his internal organs. He stopped and teetered before falling backwards landing on his seat and then toppling backwards. Even then he raised his head to look at Bill, who was scrambling to his feet with his face a mask of hate. He struggled to bring the sword in to play again but the light in his eyes faded and he slumped back dead, his sword fell from his hand. Bill was already moving forward, looking for the next opponent.

A few minutes later, the skirmish was finished. Dead and dying and wounded lay around; shaking with the after effects of an adrenaline rush Bob returned to where he had last seen his hat, It lay on the floor with the top inch and a half almost severed from the main body – that had been a close thing. He wondered if his hair had actually been cut. He ran his fingers through his hair, but soaked with sweat it was difficult to tell. He picked the hat up to examine it more closely. The cut betrayed the incredible sharpness of the sword, it was not ragged at all. He put it back on his head reasoning that he could sew it later. The top hung comically to one side, but would do for the time being until he could stitch it.

As he stepped away he came to the body of the Japanese officer. There was a huge red stain on the front of his uniform. His eyes had rolled back only the whites being visible. Bob tried to avoid looking at the officer's face, who's cloth cap with it's gold star badge was lying a couple of feet away from his head where it had rolled. The sword lay just beneath his left hand. Bob was able to pick it up without touching the body. He felt the weight and balance of it and was surprised that the handle was bound with chords and inlaid with brass chrysanthemums, rather than wood as he'd imagined. The scabbard was tucked into the officers brown leather belt rather than attached to the straps hanging from the belt. Bob guessed that it was more secure to carry it in this way in battle. He put down his rifle within easy reach and pulled the scabbard, clad in brown leather to match the belt, free and slid the sword into it. It barely made a sound until the brass hand protector touched the top of the scabbard throat. He drew it partially and noticed a near lack of sound. He put it back in and this time pulled it out again as fast he could, again, very little noise – it certainly wasn't the schinnnng! noise that always accompanied the drawing of swords at the movies. It would make a brilliant souvenir he thought, but was it worth the effort of carrying it through the jungle? He decided to try it and tucked it awkwardly into his webbing over his shoulder where he hoped it wouldn't rub too much as he walked. Finally he located the body with his embedded kukri, grabbed the handle, then as he pulled it free he looked away so as not to see the gaping, obscene gash, again without looking he wiped the blade clean on the dead Jap's shirt before returning it to the scabbard on his hip.

Bob Helen took a deep breath, and blew it out through his mouth.

He closed his eyes and shook his head as if to get rid of the memory. He picked up a rag and wiped the blade clean again, this time of oil. Then he dropped the rag back where it had come from on the bench, put the oil and stone back, picked up the torch and walked back into the house.

"You're not going to chop the carrots for me then Dear?" said his wife as he passed back through the lounge. Above the settee that she sat on hung the Samurai sword in it's leather scabbard.
Bob looked at it, then at the blade in his hand and once again remembered what he had used it for. "Errr.. I don't think I could eat carrots chopped with this Love." he smiled.

Chapter 20 – Fairy town

At first Daniel had sat down and refused to budge, so the fairy just dragged him. He was being dragged along backwards on his backside by his wrists, it meant that a lot of pressure was put on his shoulders which felt like they were being pulled out of their sockets. He screamed and writhed until he managed to swivel around so that he was dragged first with his hands under his backside which was still painful. He managed to pull his knees up and with a supreme effort thrust his feet through the gap in his arms. Once he achieved this he was being still being dragged but at least the pressure was off his shoulders and now it was only his wrists which were agony, so he carried on squealing and shouting or dear life. He saw a tree approaching, and took his chance, he rolled onto his right side and hooked his feet backwards around the trunk. The rope jerked his arms and the bark dug into his bare legs but the fairy was pulled a little off balance. He had been ready for that and yanked his arms back as hard as he could. It worked! The fairy tottered backwards and before he could regain his balance Daniel was on his feet and swinging his fists, still tied together, in a double handed blow which knocked the fairy flat, in a moment Daniel was on top of him. He didn't court fights at school, and he knew better than to get into a brawl with Angela, who being a girl could not be punched by a boy, but he could fight like one and wasn't past fighting dirty either, which is where he'd learned from and it was exactly what Daniel did now. He kicked the fairy hard in the ribs as he lay on his back. The fairy squealed with a mixture of rage, hatred and pain and reached for it's knife, which after disappearing when Daniel was coaxed into the tunnel, at some point had reappeared on the fairy's belt. As he pulled it free of it's sheath Daniel kicked instinctively at the hand that held it and with another squeal of pain the knife flew from the fairy's grasp. Daniel's temper was really up now. The fairy may have been faster, and stronger, but Daniel was a match size wise, had a weight advantage and had the fairy on the floor which put the fairy at a real disadvantage. Now Daniel pressed that disadvantage to it's maximum and stamped hard on one of the delicate wings which was stretched across the ground. Unwittingly he had found a real weakness in his foe's defences, this time the fairy shrieked, it snatched up a handful of dirt and leaf mould off the floor and flung it in Daniels face. Daniel yelled out and instinctively raised his tethered hands to his face, wiping his eyes, as he wiped most things, with his cuffs. By the time he had his vision back the fairy was gone from sight. He whirled around looking in all directions, and in the gloom he saw the knife on the floor, he checked around once more then crouched and grabbed it with both hands. He selected the largest tree that he could find and leaned back against it so that he could not be ambushed from behind and set to trying to cut through the rope without slicing into himself. It was harder than it looked in the movies, the knife was sharp but awkward to manoeuvre and use with any force. He dropped it and jumped to try and avoid it hitting his legs. He picked it up and this time managed to wedge it handle first with it's jewelled hilt in a fork in a branch, gently so as not to dislodge it he started to saw the binding back and forward on the blade. It took a few minutes but he managed it, and at last he was able to release the pressure on his wrists which suddenly ached as blood pumped through them properly again. He hissed through his teeth and rubbed them vigorously, looking round for the fairy all the while – there was no sign of it anywhere. He picked up the knife again and tested it for heft. Crudely made but actually quite well balanced. The copper blade looked funny, but the green jewel in the hilt was quite nice. Daniel wondered if the jewel was valuable. If he ever got back home, maybe he could prise it out and give it to his mom. He gripped the knife hard in his hand, wondering what to do now. He'd beaten the fairy in a fight and had a weapon, but now he still had no idea where he was, and although he hadn't been dragged that far he couldn't even see the cliff with the cave between the trees. There were drag marks on the floor, so he followed them for want of anything better to do.

Up above in a tree the fairy watched with slitted golden eyes. It had been hurt and shocked but not badly injured. It was however too shaken to make another attack at the moment, especially now that Daniel had a knife. It watched Daniel move away through the trees and then after a few minutes it flew off in another direction – slightly wonkily on account of one of its wings being bruised.

Daniel heard the fairy depart and looked around but it was too far away to see in the whispey trees. He stood still instinctively, looking in the direction that the sound seemed to have come from, listening but he heard nothing else apart form the thumping of his own heart and his breathing. After a while he turned to go on his way and jumped a little. A thin mist had come from somewhere. It was thicker on the ground and thinned as it approached the tops of the trees. He could still see the ground but visibility seemed to be about twenty yards, although being an eight year old boy Daniel couldn't have known that; it just seemed quite thick to him. Quite thick, not very thick though. He'd seen pea-soupers at home when you could feel the soot particles on your tongue and barely see your hand in front of your face, so he wasn't overly concerned, indeed maybe it would hide him from the fairy a bit better. As a bonus he found another stick on the ground, thin, but fairly stiff and strong. He reasoned it might make a better weapon than the knife as it had a longer reach so after a bit of thought he put the knife in his jacket pocket, in a way that hopefully wouldn't allow it to cut through the material and set off again.

Before long he came across a path. It was quite broad path,

similar, but much wider than the path that had led him through the hawthorn tunnel and into the wood, some hours earlier – well it seemed like a few hours, but he really wasn't sure to be honest, there didn't seem to be any real measure of time in this place and thinking about it was confusing.

He stood looking at the path, it went from left to right in front of him, straight as a die for as far as he could see in the mist. Logic dictated that he should have crossed it on the way in, but he knew he hadn't. He felt that he should turn left to find his way out again, but if he had got his bearings wrong somehow then he was actually facing the wrong way. That seemed about right and explained why he hadn't come across this road before. That being settled in his mind he therefore turned right.

Every so often he stopped and listened, but the forest was silent on both sides. The path had widened steadily and was now about the width of a road. The cobbles of which it was made seemed more worn and shinier with less moss in between them. Daniel was reminded of railway tracks which on the main lines were very shiny and on lesser used lines were duller. He guessed that this meant that the road was well used. With this in mind he walked at first on the edge of the path and then slightly off to one side, but he quickly found the ground at the sides marshy, with smelly mud, and spiky marsh grass. Not wishing to lose a shoe, he decided to risk the edge of the road, besides it made faster time. He seemed to be making good time walking briskly and using the stick as a walking staff.

Eventually something loomed out of the mist on either side of the road. It was wall made from the same stone as the cobbles beneath his feet, just in bigger rough blocks and chunks. It stood in places about eight feet tall although it had a tumbled down appearance that meant at one point in the short distance that was visible in the fog it was down to three feet. Above the road it formed an arch the stones of which were finished in a better fashion, although they were still crude.

That settled it. He hadn't come this way on the way in, so he must be going the wrong way, downhearted he went to retrace his steps and wondered how long it would take to get out of this dreary place. All at once he heard a noise of feet approaching from the other side of the arch. He stepped quickly and quietly to the side and moved towards the wall, squatting down and pressing his back against it a few feet form the archway. A few seconds later the fairy flew through the archway, he was flying slowly and slightly erratically a foot or so above the road. It hardly seemed worth the effort of not walking to Daniel who froze and clutched his stick tightly. A few yards behind him the owners of the footsteps came into view. Eight more fairies; well he presumed they were fairies, they were heavier set than the flying fairy although about the same height, they had no wings and over their green tunics they had dirty coppery looking armoured breastplates, and equally dirty looking helmets of a variety of shapes, styles and sizes. They were obviously a military squad of some sort because they were in two columns of four, but they walked rather that marched in step. Some carried sticks with copper axe or spear heads, others had swords on their belts and one carried a large wooden mallet which looked, from the split and battered ends, like it had seen plenty of use. Daniel froze, and remained frozed until long after the sound of feet on cobbles had faded into the mist.

Daniel considered his options. Returning up the road now seemed like a bad idea, there were fairies up there. Fairies who were looking for him – that much was obvious, and worse they were armed with a variety of nasty looking weapons, when all he had was a stout stick in his hand and a little knife in his pocket. Continuing along the road seemed a better option in the short run, even if it probably was the wrong direction. If the fairies weren't there then it was obviously a safer place – unless there were other fairies, more fairies, possibly with bigger, even worse weapons. There was a snort of sorts from the other side of the wall. Not loud, but indicative of someone else through the arch. Now it seemed he was caught between the devil and the deep blue sea. A squad of armed fairies one way and, well, something the other way. It seemed unlikely that the 'something' was a good something.

He wasn't keen on moving parallel to the wall as he could see that the ground still looked swampy and dangerous, indeed as he looked he saw a frog move in the grass and plop into some water where it bobbed back up and regarded him with two golden eyes which peeped above the water. He looked along the wall and another option offered itself. Carefully and quietly he walked along the edge of the wall a few yards, managing to keep his feet dryish until he came to the section of wall that was reduced to three feet in height. He peered around and over the gap, and saw nothing except an area of grass with the odd tree of the same spindly type as seemed to be the norm round here, the mist or fog appeared to continue on the other side of the wall. He tested the rocks that made up the walls construction. Some on the top seemed to be loose so he removed them and added them to the pile of already fallen rocks that he was standing on at the base of the gap. The wall was about three feet thick and easily traversed. He climbed down and sent a rock about the size of his fist rolling and clattering down the pile. He froze and waited for something to happen. Nothing did. After a while he let out his breath. Now that he was over and squatting safely on the grass – it was the measliest grass he'd ever seen – he looked back and forward and saw a poorly built stone structure about the size of a small, low-set garden shed built against the wall just short of the archway. There was another snort. There being no windows or any other sizeable openings visible he decided to get closer. Creeping up he was finally able to peer through a small gap between the stones in the structure's rear wall. He could make out a figure seated in an open doorway facing away from him. The figure, obviously another fairy of the armour wearing type snorted again and Daniel relaxed as he realised he was hearing snores. Ah! A Sentry hut. The fairy was leaning to one side with a spear resting on it's shoulder. Daniel could see the tip pointing in his general direction, and moving up and down in time to the fairy's breathing. He toyed with the idea of walking round and stealing the spear. He thought he could do it without waking the fairy, but what if he did wake up? Well Daniel had already scrapped with one fairy and beaten him up, why not another? Well, this one looked stronger and was wearing armour. Best leave it to sleep. He yawned himself, realising it had been some time since he had slept, in fact the last time would be just before he woke up this morning and cleared out of the house before Angela could put her shoe on and find the worm he'd put in there. A realisation hit him. When he had looked in through the mirror in the cave and seen his mom and sister in the back room with the two police officers the room had been lit by gas light, he was certain of that, which meant it must have been dark when he was viewing them.

He had been roaming around for some time since then, hours maybe. It must have been later than he thought, but it didn't make any real sense. He thought back to the time he had been late back for dinner after dallying with the fairy for a few minutes, time seemed to move differently here, but to an eight year old who really only had the most rudimentary grasp of how fast time passed in the real world, a different speed of time didn't really make any sense. He put his mind back to the current situation in hand and crept back to the road and headed away from the guard post.

The road wound in and out in sweeping curves, the trees had returned on wither side and he walked along at their edge using them for cover. There was a gradual incline as the road climbed a hill at the top he paused. The mist cleared and the trees stopped. About fifty yards away in a natural bowl was a collection of hovels, all of them several times larger than the sentry post at the wall, and two in particular were much larger, but even so perhaps only the size of a medium sized house. They were built in the fashion of elongated igloos, but using stones instead of ice blocks. There appeared to be no windows to speak of in the buildings, although he could see doorways with what looked like curtains covering the openings form the inside. He stepped into the trees so as not to be seen and counted the buildings. There seemed to be about twenty of them. If each one housed a fairy that made twenty faires. Eight fairies had walked off looking for him, that left twelve fairies. One flying fairy had gone with them, that left eleven and one asleep by the arch in the guard hut, that left ten fairies to deal with, but that did assume only one fairy per building. What of there was a family of fairies in each house? There were after all three people living in his house and about eight in the Steptoe's house. His mom had said that Mrs Steptoe popped babies out at the same speed that most people popped peas out of a pod. He wasn't sure exactly how you popped a baby out, but the metaphor had seemed funny when he'd heard her discussing it with one of the neighbours on the doorstep one day. A day which seemed so long ago.

He observed the village, if that was what it was, or some time whilst wondering what to do. He noted that whilst the road appeared to go through the houses the houses were not actually adjoined to the road as at home, there were no paved footpaths, just muddy looking patches to and from the doors of the buildings, and there appeared to be smoke from rudimentary chimneys from eight of the buildings. The smoke rose vertically into the gloomy sky without any deviation to indicate the slightest hint of a breeze. At the far side of the village was something that might have been a well. It was a small circular wall, but it lacked the traditional pitched roof which he expected of a well, however the presence of a bucket and a rope on top of the circular wall did seem to suggest that it was indeed a well. Seeing it made him realise that he was thirsty again. Also he needed to relieve himself. He walked a little further into the trees and did just that.

Once finished, he made his way back to a position where he could see the village again, and despite only having moved a few yards he became disorientated and it took a while to find the village again. In the end he blundered out of the woods and more by luck than judgement found the village in front of him. A wingless fairy was no more than thirty yards in front of him, but by luck it was facing away from him. He had come almost a third of the way around the village and was much lower and closer to the level of the village than he had been when he had first spied the settlement. The fairy was heading in the direction of the well and was carrying a rough pottery pot under one arm, it was about twice the size of the bucket, in the other hand was a staff which it used as a walking stick, in the same manner as Daniel had used the stick he carried. Once at the well it put the pot on the ground, bent down and picked up a chain that lay there. He yanked hard on the chain and there was a squawk, which made him snigger. He yanked again and from the other side of the well a figure rose up and staggered toward him impelled by the chain which was attached to a collar around it's neck. At first he thought it was another fairy, but the build and the way it moved were wrong. It was filthy, but he realised it was wearing a dress and what had once been a blouse. The hair was long and matted, but indisputably it was a little girl.

"No sleeping!" Snarled the fairy and fetched the girl a whack across the head with it's stick, "Get me water!"
The girl squealed and dropped to the floor. She tried to cover her head and at the same time scramble to her feet.
"Get me water! Fill the pot!", the fairy yanked the chain again and was so intent on tormenting it's victim that it never noticed Daniel. In one hand he had his stick, in the other the stone that had been in his pocket since he had pried it free in the pit. Having checked for other fairies and crept up to the well he had intended to smash the stone into the fairies skull, but found despite his rage at seeing someone, or something, hitting and maltreating a girl he couldn't bring himself to do it. Instead he threw the stone hard at the bucket which fell clattering and bouncing down the well, which seemed very deep. The fairy stopped and looked at the well puzzled. It stepped forward and looked over the edge as a splosh from a long way down indicated the presence of water. Daniel swung his stick at the fairy's back, thankful that this one wasn't wearing armour. The fairy staggered forward with a stifled cry and steadied itself with both hands on the wall. Before it could recover Daniel grasped it's ankles and yanked upwards, the fairy was forced to dive head first into the well, it shrieked but there was a thud as its head stuck the side of the well and it made no

more sound before a colossal splash echoed up the well. Daniel looked around frantically, but no other fairies seemed to have heard or noticed anything. He looked at the girl who was looking back at him with mouth agape and eyes wide – not to mention crossed.

"Who are you?" she whispered.

Daniel managed to smile and say, "I'm Daniel. But you can call me Dan or Danny, I don't mind which. I'm here to rescue you. How do we get that chain off you?"

They struggled with the chain for several minutes to no avail, then Daniel remembered the knife in his pocket. All the time Emily, who's name he had ascertained, chattered away at ten to the dozen, despite being told to be quiet several times in case they were heard. None of her chattering went into Daniel's head as he frantically tried to free her. He put the knife to the collar which was a leather strap fastened by the last link of the chain which was made of rough thick copper links. The leather, despite being thick and stout, was cut through in a moment.

Daniel grasped her hand and pulled her to follow him in the direction of the road again.

"Where are you going?" she asked.

"Home I hope. That one with the wings kidnapped me, but I'm not sure of the way."

"Well there's more than one with wings, and that's the wrong way." She said. "The only thing in that direction is the tombs. When one of them dies they made me bury them under a pile of rocks. You need to follow the road back the other way then paths branch off to all parts of the world where they have secret doors. You have to know which path to follow or you never get home. They told me that when I got away once and they caught me, they said even if I found a secret door, I'd never open it and even if I did it could be anywhere in the world and I'd never get home."

"How many tombs have you built? They don't sound much like proper tombs like King Tutankhamen? How long have you been here?"

"Weeks I think. Mater and Pater will be frantic, but thank you for rescuing me. I don't know who King whatever his name is, but I know all the Kings and Queens of England and he isn't one of them. I've built two tombs, they sometimes die in our world, then the others have to go and get the body. The first one had a jagged wound, he'd been killed by a lump of iron and they don't like iron, they had to get it out of his body before they could bring him back. The other one had his wings pulled off and had been thrown in the river, it took them ages to find him. They weren't happy and took it out on me. They'd both gone out to kidnap children and died before they could get any, So I'm the only one here, and have to do all the work. I'm so tired."

Billy looked at her and suddenly she did look exhausted.

"They don't let you sleep." she said.

"Well we can't sleep now." he replied, "We have to get away."

"Yes, I suppose we must." she replied, "But how will we ever find the way."

"I don't know but we'll find a way. Maybe we can kidnap one and make them show the way."

How can you not know about King Tutankhamen? He thought to himself.

Chapter 21 - The Invasion of fairyland

"So you don't think I'm mad then?" Asked PC Helen

"No." replied Sergeant Richmond.

"There's something you're not telling me then."

"There's a lot I'm not telling you."

"It might be helpful if you did tell me Sergeant."

The two men had left Bob Helen's house in uniform with their helmets and capes, which hid Bob's kukri. On Bill Richmond's instructions Bob had packed a small rucksack with some items including a flask of hot tea.

"Tea. Really?"

"We might be gone some time." said Bill Richmond as they headed toward the park."

"We're going to the park, yes?"

"To start with."

"Well, there are houses fifty yards away, I dare say we could cadge a cup somewhere." Bob jibed.

"Not the part of the park we're going to."

"Seriously, flask of tea, kukri for cutting branches, torch etcetera. I'm guessing we're staking out somewhere. That creature I saw in Borneo... The fairy. You know where there is one around here don't you? So we catch the little blighter and get Daniel's location from him?

"You're close Constable."

"We're police officers, but how does the law relate to this creature, if it exists? I mean can we arrest something that patently isn't human?"

"Oh it exists," Said Bill, "Or at least I think it does. I've seen them twice, well I think I have."

Bob looked at Bill, "Go on?"

"Last time was on the retreat from Mons. I was on a cart being used as an ambulance. I dived off when I heard a shell coming in. I came face to face with one which had been been killed by a previous shell, but the first time; the first time was in the park the year before the queen died, it tried to tempt me into following down a tunnel in the hawthorn bush. When that didn't work it tried to drag me. My boots saved me."

"Your boots?"

"Yes, they were hob nailed and the moment they touched the cobbles on the path in the tunnel everything vanished, tunnel, fairy, everything. They don't like iron for some reason."

"Yeah, that one in Borneo. That was being tortured with iron. The head hunter said it was saying that the knife burned it. But if there's a tunnel, shouldn't we have bought spades?

"Eh?"

"Spades to dig down and find the tunnel."

"Oh, I see." said Bill, "Not that kind of tunnel, it's actually inside the hawthorn bush?"

"Bill," Bill gave him a look." "Sorry. Sergeant, I promise you it isn't in the bush. There's nothing in there, I went in and Humphries met me in the middle. There's nothing there."

"You need a special key to get in."

"A special key?" asked Bob in a voice which expressed not a little doubt.

"Well, it's not really a key, but it works as one to open a hidden door."

"I see. And do you know where we can get one of these keys?"

"There's one in my pocket, at least that's what I hope it is. Remember I told you about the one I found in Belgium?"

"Yes."

"Well, I lifted it off his body. It was war booty – you know what soldiers are like for lifting souvenirs?"

"No sergeant, theft is theft and I'm a policeman, I don't know what you're talking about sergeant. Honest."

"Ha! So where did that Nip sword on your lounge wall come from then?"

"Oh, I won that fair and square." laughed Bob.

"Sure you did."

"I did. Me and this Jap officer had a little competition – he lost – I got his sword as a prize."

"Oh. I see." said Bill, catching on. "Well, this thing that I've got was a war souvenir." he pulled the knife out of his pocket in its sheath and handed it to Bob Helen.

"It was only later while I was recuperating from my wound that I realised, or more correctly remembered, that I'd watched the fairy I'd seen in the park use one to open the tunnel. I'm hoping that this Belgian one will work in a British setting. If not then it's going to be a short night's work."

"That one you saw as a lad?"

"Yes?"

"You mentioned a young girl going missing, I'm guessing you think the two are connected?"

Bill Richmond stopped walking and his head dropped and shoulders slumped. "I'm certain of it." He continued walking.

"She was never found?"

"Emily? No. Vanished without a trace."

"In that case, if you're right, and assuming that it's still the same fairy, we're looking for a child killer." His voice hardened. After a pause "It's not your fault you know sergeant?"

"What isn't?"

"Emily being taken?"

"What?! What the hell makes you think that I think it is my fault constable? Who the hell are you, Sigmund Freud?"

"Actually it was your body language. I've seen the reactions of enough people who've lost friends and comrades in battle and blamed themselves."

Bill didn't say anything until they reached the park gates a few minutes later, then he stopped and looked Bob square in the eye. "It was my fault. If I'd kept my trap shut about what I'd seen she might still be here. I didn't tell her where the fairy was, and I warned her it was dangerous, but she must've figured it out somehow."

"Do you seriously think that if it had tried to grab you, and Emily hadn't shown up it could've gone away Sergeant? Do you? It would have just waited and grabbed another child. There was nothing a little kid could have done. What were you're options? Tell the local Bobby? You'd have got the same thick ear you'd give a kid who came telling tales today."

"That bit's true Bob, you should've met PC Grisdale, he was mean; used to go on the beat reeking of gin – and heaven help anyone who messed him around."

"It's all true sergeant. And the reason I brought it up is because we're police officers and we enforce the law – the moment we allow it to get personal then we stop being professional. I'm not talking about giving some lowlife a hiding to teach them the error of their ways rather than clog the cells and courts up. I'm talking about revenge, we can't do that."

Bill looked at him, long, cold and hard.

"What are you saying? We arrest a fairy? That's going to be interesting before the beak. Would it even be subject to our laws? We need to find a way to be sure that it can't harm another kid. Emily wasn't the first."

"What?" said Bob.

"There's a pattern; every forty nine years a child goes missing, as far back as I can find. Daniel, Emily in 1900, Enid Bradbury before her and the one previous was the last Marquis's son. I've been with the vicar this afternoon going through the church records – we only went back three hundred years and every forty nine years we found a child's name – missing presumed dead, missing, taken by persons unknown, stolen or just plain missing. The records actually go back into the 1500's but they started on lose sheets of paper or parchment and are knee deep in dust."

"Three hundred years – six kids?"

"Seven if you include Daniel. I'm sure if we'd looked at the sheets there'd have been more, and this parish has a longer history than that. It's in the Domesday book as a hamlet, although at that time it wasn't called Beare-in-the-Green, it was called 'Bearnbygren', or something. The vicar tells me that's Anglo Saxon. Care to have a stab at it's meaning?"

"Something to do with green fairies, I'd guess?"

"You'd be wrong. It means 'Child's grave' or possibly 'burial place of the children.'"

Bob felt an icicle slide down his spine. "That's... That's an awful lot of kids. Nine hundred years? Does the vicar know what we're doing?" he wiped at a tear that was pricking the corner of his eye with his tunic sleeve. If Bill noticed he didn't say anything.

"At least nine hundred years. And yes, he knows what I'm doing. I'd just got back in when you rang."

"You were going on your own?"

"Yes. I didn't expect you to believe me. The good reverend offered to come, but I asked him to stop here and pray, when you rang I think it was an answer to prayer."

"I'd have thought the vicar might have been useful to come along actually," said Bob, "We could be looking at something supernatural. A man of God might be useful. Is it too late to fetch him?"

"Yes, he might be, and I regret not bringing him, but in fairness he lost a leg when his tank was hit by a shell from an eighty-eight at El Alemaign. He was up for it, but I know he's had trouble with the wooden one rubbing. Trust me, he's doing his bit at the vicarage. Besides if we don't come back someone needs to explain things."

Bob was silent for a minute. He hadn't considered not coming back when he'd left the house less than half an hour ago. After a while he said, "Well, I really don't know how he's going to explain this. And I had no idea he was military. He didn't wear any medals at the cenotaph on Remembrance Sunday."

"Oh he's got them, including a Military Cross, for pulling someone out of a burning tank at Tobruk, he just doesn't talk about them. No, he's a man of peace now, which is why I don't think he'd really approve of these."

He pulled something from under his cape and held it out. Bob couldn't see it in the dark but his hand closed on the butt of a revolver.

"It is loaded."

"Don't I have to sign for this?" Bob asked.

"Not tonight." There was a wry smile from the sergeant. "I wouldn't know what to put in the book as a reason for getting them out of the armoury."

"I've never carried a gun as a Bobby; No grenades, I suppose?" Grinned Bob.

"Ha ha, sorry we're fresh out."

"Pity. I like grenades. I've often thought we could use them on the beat for breaking up pub brawls on a weekend." grinned Bob. He tucked the pistol; a .38 Smith and Wesson into his belt.

"Let's go then."

They found the gates locked again and used the same entrance that had sufficed last time. Very soon they stood before the hawthorn bush.

"Well, how does this 'key' of yours work?"

In silence Bill produced the knife, which was really too small for his hand. He took it from it's scabbard and pushed it into the Hawthorn, it was a few seconds before anything could be seen to be happening, but slowly and surely a hole was forming."

"That's... unusual." said Bob watching the hawthorn strands slowly and imperceptibly reforming on what seemed to be the periphery of his vision.

"Point that pistol through that hole." Bob whispered.

Bob drew his revolver and crouched to get a better view past Bill.

After a couple of minutes a dimly lit tunnel was visible. Since they were stood in darkness it actually seemed quite light to the two policemen, and they could clearly see that there was nothing presenting itself as a target.

"I've got a bad feeling about this." said Bob.

They crept into the tunnel walking bent over due to the height, Bill led, having sheathed and pocketed the fairy blade and drawn his revolver instead, He glanced down at the cobbles on the floor as he went and noticed small pock marks on two of them. They looked like they'd been burned into the stone and he guessed, correctly as it happened, that they might have been from the hob nails on his boots a life time ago. They turned the corner of the tunnel and suddenly found themselves in a rather murky forest of spindly trees. They stood a while getting their bearings and getting used to the strange scent of the place, musty and slightly intoxicating.

"Well, looking at this lot I don't think we'll need that kukri of yours after all." Said Bill.

"On the contrary." said Bob, he opened his tunic and put the pistol inside – a safer option than sticking it in his belt. That done he reached round and drew the kukri from it's scabbard, which was properly attached to his belt. He swung the blade easily twice and took a small but quite visible pale looking chunk out of the trunk nearest to the tunnel. The tree shook and trembled, Bob moved across to the other side of the tunnel mouth and repeated his action, again the tree trembled, almost shuddered.

"Even the trees don't like the touch of iron." Bill said, "Good idea though, I think you could get lost in this place quite easily.

"Every twenty yards?"

"Sounds about right." said Bob. "We could follow this path but it fades in and out, and I can see spore, but it looks like it's been here a while and it's not particularly clear, so I think it's a good precaution. Besides if it attracts a bit of attention I reckon we could grab a prisoner.

They had gone about a mile by the reckoning of counting the number of trees Bob had chipped, when Bob stopped dead and listened. "There's that attention we wanted. We're being followed." he murmured. In quiet places a murmur is much quieter than a whisper.

Bill listened carefully with him and after a minute or so in the distance there came the definite snap of a branch underfoot.

"That's the third time." Bob muttered.

Wordlessly he motioned to a bush that was large enough and just about thick enough to conceal two burly coppers. Bob slid the kukri into its scabbard and drew his truncheon. Bill nodded, they were after all still policemen and gestured that he would use his pistol as a back up.

Eventually they heard small noises that indicated that who or whatever it was that was tailing them was almost upon their ambush, but then they stopped. A voice, quiet and yet with a certain command to it spoke.

"Are you there Bill?"

Both policemen froze, then Bob looked quizzically at Bill. Who turned the corners of his mouth down and raised his eyebrows. Both officers jumped, but avoided the ignominy of shouting out as a human head popped round the bush. "Ah there you are, and you've bought PC Helen too. Good, good."

"Reverend Whetherby! What in hell's name are you doing here?" Bill hissed.

The reverend looked hurt "Nothing in hell's name I hope. More in Heaven's name as is suited to my calling."

"How long have you been following us reverend?"

"Oh, well, let me see. I didn't follow you from the vicarage, because I knew where you'd be going so I went to the park. Do you know I had to squeeze through a gap in the fence? Most undignified, and I hid in a bush. Unfortunately I had a bit of a doze and you were already entering the tunnel as I woke up. I waited for a while by the entrance for a minute or two, and then it seemed to be closing up again, so I nipped through smartish. I followed the marks you left on the trees, but I really have to say that it a real inconvenience trying to follow the marks from the wrong side."

"Can't you tell he was an officer?" Snorted Bill, starting to chuckle.

"Hmm, yes." Said the vicar. He was wearing a black suit and shirt with his white dog collar. In his right hand he held a walking stick made of ash, with a silver knob on top. He put his hand into the outside left pocket of the jacket and pulled out a leather hip flask, which he opened and offered to Bill, "I know rankers and NCO's prefer rum, but being an ex-officer I only have sherry, would you like a nip or do you feel it's above your station sergeant?"

Bob almost kept a straight face, almost, "He's on duty I'm afraid Vicar." he sniggered.

Bill glared at him. "I'll remember that next time you're sinking a quite pint after hours in a pub PC Helen."

Bob looked innocent. "Which pub would that be sergeant?" he asked.

"Would you like the full list Constable?"

"We could say that the sherry was communion wine?" said Bill

"No we could not!" the vicar said. "Firstly we need bread for communion, or wafers – did you know the choir boys call them 'Jesus biscuits?' - shocking! Secondly it's not consecrated and thirdly, if word ever got out out the parishioners would want it at every communion. St Bart's can't afford that – do you know how much the parish share is? They'll have to make do with cheap wine, watered down I'm afraid"

"I don't even know what a parish share is." said Bob

"It's the money every parish pays to the diocese to get a vicar and keep the bishop in the luxury to which he is accustomed etcetera." He took a nip of the sherry. Bob held out his hand and the vicar gave him the flask. "Mm, I could get used to this."

"Not at St. Bart's by the sound of it." Grumbled Bill and took a turn himself before handing it back.

"Thank you vicar, that's pretty good actually."

"How did you know we were here vicar?" asked Bob.

"Well, I heard the chopping stop, so I guessed you were stood still. So every time I came to a piece of suitable cover, I called. Eventually I came to the right one. Simple really."

"You're lucky I didn't shoot you creeping us on us like that vicar." Said Bill.

"Hmpf! You wouldn't be the first to shoot at me, and what have you got? Is that a .38"? Well I've survived being shot at with a German 88mm anti tank gun so your pea-shooter doesn't worry me too much." the vicar grinned. Shall we go? We really could do with finding Daniel if he's still with us."

Chapter 22 Daniel and Emily

They had exited the village, if it could be called that, without incident creeping around the tree line whilst making sure that they could see the buildings so that they didn't lose heir sense of direction. Emily confirmed that getting lost was really easy.

"I've tried to escape several times and each time I've got lost in the woods. They don't look like anything really, but it's like a maze without walls, as soon as you loose sight of something it's like it moves. I'm sure that it moves, you wind up walking round and round in circles."

"Like a Teddy bear?" quipped Daniel, who was still ecstatic to have found a friendly face even if Emily was a chatter box and the chances of being crept up on by a fairy were greatly increased by this.

"A what?"

"A teddy bear?"

Emily looked at him with a quizzical expression.

"Round and round the garden, like a teddy bear?"

"I'm sorry I'm not following what it is you mean."

"You must know what a teddy bear is?"

Daniel checked around, realising that he had been distracted by the conversation, so he made sure that he could still see the road and that nothing was following them.

"I'm afraid I don't." Said Emily looking puzzled.

Daniel wasn't sure what to make of that. He didn't think Emily was lying, what would be the point, but how could you possibly not know about teddy bears?"

"Where are you from Emily?"

"Ermm. A village,"

"What's it called?"

"Beare-in-the-Green, it's in the county of Staffordshire."

"Really? That's where I come from? Where abouts do you live? I live on Cardigan Road."

"Oh, the new houses? I live in Victoria Avenue."

"Oh, the posh end? And my road isn't new. Mom and Dad lived there before the war."

"Which war? Was that the one in Africa – Mate-bele-land?" She struggled over the pronunciation.

"Where? I don't know that one. It's not part of the Empire is it? I know all the countries I think. And not that war, the second world war."

"Where's the second world? I've only heard of the Old world and the New World."

Daniel was shocked.

"Which school do you go to Emily?"

"The one just round the corner from the church in the High Street."

"That's my school too – I thought you looked familiar."

"I don't think I've ever seen you before Daniel, but I am very glad to have met you now."

"Well I know I've seen your face before somewhere."

Emily's face dropped. "Do you mean my squint?" She sounded hurt.

"No, not that." Said Daniel blushing. "I just know I've seen your face before. It must've been at school. Who is your teacher?"

"Well it was Miss Ball, but after the incident in the ladies room we had Mr. Ramsey. Do you know if Miss Ball is back yet – we were all hoping she'd stay away for ever and not come back."

"I don't know any of those staff." said Daniel. He wondered if there was another school around another corner from the church that he didn't know about.

"Well you must know Mr. Ramsey. He's the headmaster, everyone knows him!"

"No, Mr. Robb is the headmaster. I should know I've been in his study three times, but I got away with it every time."

"Don't be silly Daniel! Mr Ramsey is the headmaster! He takes the assembly most mornings, and he had everyone in the whole school in an assembly just the other week and roared at us because someone did something to Miss Ball while she was doing her business."

Daniel was uneasy. He knew there were three primary schools in the area but neither of the other two were anywhere near the church. In fact one of them was in an outlying village, and the other was a mile away from the church and the High Street. He had a vague recollection of the name Ramsey on the wooden board of previous headmasters names in the entrance of the school, but he couldn't be sure as he never paid any real attention to it. It didn't make sense. So he persisted.

"Which shop is opposite the school gate?"

"Mr Jupp's shop of course."

"Ohh.", Well it was the butcher's shop owned by Mr Jupp. Mr Jupp was a nice chap, who's son worked for him and who's grandson was the delivery boy. The money at the counter was still taken by Mr. Jupp's mother who was in her eighties and had been doing the job since her husband, now deceased, had worked there for his father.

"So this Miss Ball, what happened to her?"

Emily stopped walking and made a point of looking around carefully to make sure that no one was listening. No one was.

"Well, she was sat there in the lady's room and I heard from my mom who knows the Constable Grisdale's wife said that someone opened the door at the back and pushed nettles up under the seat."

Daniel didn't understand how or where the door in back of the WC was, or how they could get nettles between the toilet seat and the rim of the porcelain toilet, even if they could get into the back of the cubicle, but he guffawed at the thought of act.

"That's so rude!" he choked.

"I think it may have been Billy Richmond, but I can't prove it, but he looked terribly guilty in the assembly, he was blushing like a beetroot."

"Is he a relative of Sgt Richmond? He'll be in trouble if he finds out."

"Sgt Richmond?"

"Yes, the police officer."

"I don't know him, only Mr. Grisdale."

Daniel gave up. "Come on." He said, "We need to get out of here. Do you know where the tunnel leading in is?"

Emily looked at him and said quietly, "I thought you knew the way? I thought you'd come to rescue me?"

"Well, I have. I got that chain off you and rescued you from the village didn't I?" He stopped suddenly and squatted down. Emily followed his gaze and did likewise. They had come to the arch in the wall, the sentry was wandering around outside of his sentry hut his spear in his hand. Fortunately, the thin vegetation they'd kept between them and the road had kept them from being noticed. The sentry's attention seemed to be fixed on something through the arch, as he paced around he kept looking through it. He was obviously on alert, possibly expecting the return of the squad which had marched through earlier, but it seemed reasonable to assume that he wasn't going to turn around any time soon.

"Come on. There's a way through." said Daniel. They advanced as close as they dared and then broke cover and quietly walked diagonally across to the gap in the wall. The sentry didn't look round once. Something had obviously rattled him though because he kept fiddling with his spear and passing it from hand to hand as he glanced through the arch. Daniel couldn't know it but the guard was merely waiting for his relief, and wondering when he would be back. Even in a realm where the passage of time is somewhat strange it is possible to get bored when you are waiting for someone to take over your shift.

Crossing back through the gap in the wall, this time Daniel was careful that neither of them made the slightest sound. The idea of following the road from a few feet inside the woods was out. The guard was too active and alert, they would have to chance the swamp.

Actually it wasn't quite as bad as Daniel had thought. Now they moved in near silence concentrating on keeping to the drier bits, marked by little tufts of spikey grass and mounds of moss. Eventually they came to drier ground, which after the swamp seemed almost cheery by comparison. They stopped for a moment and Emily looked down at her feet. Her shoes were in a poor state of repair and as she wiggled her toes muddy water squelched out from them. She stood there and smiled at Daniel,
"My Mater is going to be so angry when she sees these."
"I think she'll be more concerned at seeing you again and too happy to be worried about a pair of shoes."

They stood there and then Emily cocked her head to one side.

"Can you hear that?"

Daniel craned his head, "Water trickling?" he said.

"Yes!" and with that Emily was away trotting through the trees. Daniel followed her and after a short distance found a slow moving stream. He wondered if it was the same stream he'd found previously. Emily stopped, and then she followed the stream against it's flow,

"Come on." she said.

A little way through the woods they came to a pool. Daniel realised that it was indeed the same place; he could see the rock face with the water flowing out of it. They walked around the edge of the pool towards it.

"Someone's been here!" said Emily looking at the footprints by the rock face.

"That was me. We can drink the water, it's quite nice."

So they did. Once they'd slaked their thirst Emily, being a lady also insisted on washing her grimy face in the clean fresh water. Lacking a towel Daniel very graciously took off his jacket and lent it to her to dry herself. She rubbed her face and smiled at him as she handed it back.

"I know where I've seen you before." said Daniel.

They were able to follow Daniel's previous tracks from the water. Daniel picked up a stick on the way and soon they came to the cave which contained the mirrors. As before they could see the light inside. Daniel grabbed Emily's hand.

"What are you doing?" She asked snatching her hand back, "I barely know you!"

"There's a pit inside in the dark, you need to keep a hold of me while I find it with my stick."

"Well in that case...", and she took his left arm. "There's no harm in you being a gentleman."

Daniel shook his head and walked into the cave with Emily on his arm. He was tapping his stick feeling for the pit which he found easily, they stepped around it and approached the first mirror.

Daniel felt very sad. "They can't hear or see you." He said, "It's like a movie that plays over and over."

"A movie?"

"Yes. This is my mom and sister."

Emily gasped, "They're showing their ankles and, and their legs too!" she squeaked.

"Why wouldn't they?" said Daniel looking at the knee length skirts. After a while PC Helen came into the picture, "That's PC Helen."

They stood watching, Daniel's heart filled with longing for hearth and home.

Eventually PC Helen was followed a short while later by Sqt Richmond. "That's Sergeant Richmond."

"Oh my gosh! He does look like Billy – they must be related, I wonder if that's his father."

"He doesn't have any children. I don't think the Sergeant ever married even." Said Daniel, and shuddered at the thought of having Sgt Richmond as a father. It did bother him not having a father, but since he had been conceived whilst his father was home on leave and his father had then been killed before Daniel had been born he had no memories of him, but the thought of a father as scary as Sgt Richmond was surely much worse.

"His uncle perhaps?"

"Perhaps." Said Daniel, "Look at this next one."

They shuffled across the floor of the cave and again Emily gasped. "It's Mater and Pater!" she began to sob, "Oh I thought I'd never see them again. They're weeping!"

"That's you in the photograph isn't it?" Asked Daniel.

"Yes that's me. I went to the studio to have it done last year." she snuffled. "Oh, it's so good to see them – can't we pass through the window to them?"

"No, it's like I said, it's like going to the pictures and watching a movie. You don't have a clue what I'm talking about do you?" This was because by the light from the mirror he could see that she was looking puzzled again.

"No, I'm afraid not."

"What was the date that you were kidnapped Emily?"

"Let me see, I think it was the 14th of March."

"What year?"

"What year? Why, Nineteen hundred of course? What other year would it have been?"

"It.... It's not nineteen hundred Emily."

"What do you mean? What year is it then?"

"It was nineteen forty nine when I left a few hours, or maybe days ago, I can't tell the time here in this place."

"No, no! It can't be! I can see Mater and Pater, please it can't be true." she went silent with shock.

Tears welled down her face. Daniel stood their silently.

Suddenly there was movement at the cave mouth. A bright light flooded in suddenly blinding them. "Daniel!"

Chapter 23 - The Reunion

"Daniel!" PC Helen repeated.

Daniel could see the tall shape of a police helmet above the glare of the torch that he held in his hand.

"Mr. Helen!" Daniel screamed with joy, "Watch out Mr Helen! There's a pit in front of you!"

PC Helen stopped dead and flicked his torch down, picking the pit out with it's beam.

"Got it. Thanks Daniel. Are you okay?"

"Yes Mr Helen! How did you find me?"

The PC came close to Daniel. For the first time ever in PC Helen's presence Daniel did not feel scared, just very, very relieved. Now he knew everything would be fine.

"We came across your tracks and followed them. Ah we wondered who you're companion was. Who are you young lady? What's you're name?"

"Emily Sir."

"Emily???"

The torch rested on her face and stayed there for several seconds.

"You'd better come out."

"Emily?" It was Sgt Richmond's voice. "Emily?"

He entered the cave. Reverend Whetherby was visible in the entrance with his back to the cave watching the surrounding clearing.

"Watch the pit Sergeant."

Sergeant Richmond advanced into the cave, reached the children and crouched to look at Emily. "How can it be you? You haven't aged?"

"I think, I think I go to school with your nephew Sergeant." she said.

"Oh Emily." Sergeant Richmond dissolved into tears and slid down the cave wall till he was sitting on the floor sobbing. "Oh Emily, please forgive me. It's me Billy! I should never have told you about the fairies! I should have kept my trap shut, I'm so sorry."

"Billy? It cant be you, how can you be so old, what happened to you?"

"It's not me Emily, it's you. You've stayed young, Time doesn't work the same in fairyland as back home."

"This isn't fairyland." Said Emily, "Those aren't fairies, they're goblins, they just tell people that they're fairies to get them to follow them."

Bob Helen, embarrassed by the sight of the tough old sergeant breaking down looked away and caught sight of the mirrors. "What the hell? That's me! What is this place?"

"I know what it is." this was Emily. "They feed on the misery of the ones the children leave behind, they told me that's what they do, but not how they did it. They must come and gaze through the windows and enjoy the sight of our parents in misery. Billy? If forty nine years have gone by then are my Mater and Pater still alive? Please tell me."

Sergeant Richmond got to his feet, he took Emily by the hand and led her towards the front of the cave. Daniel followed. Outside they were met by Reverend Wetherby, who hugged Daniel and then Emily.

"So you're Emily?" he said. She nodded. "Mater and Pater?" she asked Bill again.

"I'm afraid they passed away some years ago Emily." Sergeant Richmond.

She nodded and her lip trembled but she didn't cry. "Are they in heaven Reverend?"

"I should hope so Emily, I should hope they are, and one day you will see them again. I never met your parents but I do understand from the Sergeant that they loved you a great deal and never gave up hope of finding you again."

"I think I will see them soon." she said.

"Oh no child, not for a good time yet, not now that we've found you, we'll take you back and you will be looked after I promise."

"No. They told me that they keep children for seven times seven years, that's forty nine. I never thought it was that long, it felt like a few weeks. After forty nine years they catch another child and then they throw you out and you die and rot to bones the very moment you get back to England, or the other places they take children from."

"What?" said the vicar in disbelief. "No, we'll find a way to protect you, that's assuming they told you the truth.". A voice in his head told him that it would explain the repeated discovery of bones in the hawthorn bush though.

"How can you protect me though?" she asked.

He looked her in the eyes. "Well, if I can't find a way then I promise you won't be left here alone. If I can't bring you with me then I'll stay with you. Do we have a deal?"

"I, I suppose so, but it's a horrible dreary place."

A noise made everyone look up. There was movement in the trees, in front of them. Bob was still in the cave and there was no time to get out of the clearing. "Back into the cave!" hissed Bill.

"What's up?" asked Bob, as they approached him.

"Something's coming. Light's out." Said Bill. The torches held by the police officers snapped out and the only light remaining came from the cave entrance and the mirrors. "Back around the corner and stay quiet." said Bob. They all complied feeling their way in the gloom. Once there Bob lay down so just his head showed around the corner – that and the hand which held the revolver. "Bill, check along the cave and see if there's a way out that way." He heard the sergeant groping his way along. "Vicar look after the kids."

"Will do."

The tension was electrifying, but at last Bob caught sight of the flying fairy – or more correctly flying goblin as it appeared in the entrance. He could hear other noises outside indicating more goblins outside, One, then two more goblins appeared behind the one hovering in the entrance, he noticed the lack of wings on their backs, and therefore concentrated on the silhouette of the flying one, drawing a bead on him. The goblin was quite close when he noticed Bob's head, it squealed in panic. A roar which was deafening and a flash of light followed by the smell of burning cordite signalled that Bob had pulled the trigger. The goblin screamed and fell to the ground, in a flash Bob was on his feet, he came round the corner like an express train pouncing on the stricken form in the dark. "Come here you!" there was a snapping of handcuffs and a shrieking from the goblin. Bob had it back around the corner before the ones at the cave entrance had recovered from the shock of the gunshot.

"It BURNS!!!!!" IT BURRRRNNNNSSSSSSSSS!!!!!" screamed the goblin, "Take it off, please take it off! It burns so! Please, please have pity, what did I ever do to you. It burns my wrists", the steel handcuffs were agonising on it's wrists.

A torch held by the vicar came on, and illuminated a writhing green figure. A small graze on it's shoulder oozed greenish looking blood.

"Shut it!" Bob smacked the goblin in it's face with a fist which while not made of iron, was as hard as. The goblin went quiet apart from an occasional whimper. Bob looked back around the corner, towards the entrance. Several goblin faces peered back at him from around the entrance. He could see their golden eyes wide and worried, but other than that they showed very little. An arm came into sight and a spear was thrown down the cave. A spear is a long stabbing weapon not a throwing weapon, that would make it a javelin, the spear head being large and heavy unbalances it when thrown. It flew down the cave and hit the floor before cartwheeling along bouncing of the surfaces of the cave before coming to rest beside Bob. He put a hand out in the darkness, felt for it, found it and grabbed it, pulling it around alongside his body. One extra weapon wouldn't go amiss.

"There's nothing up there apart from a load of those window things. That's the only way out of this place." Announced Bill as he returned. Then, "Well, well, well, what - have - we - got – here?" this was to the goblin who lay trembling on the floor. "Don't remember me do you?"
"I remember you – Sam!"
"Yeah, that's me! But I lied, My name is Bill. You can call me sergeant Richmond!" He reached down and grabbed the goblin by the throat, lifting it clear off the ground, it writhed and wriggled as Bill's fingers gripped it's windpipe. "How many kids, you little swine?" he snarled, "How many? I can't count the windows down that passage and in everyone I see weeping parents."
"Please don't kill him sergeant." This was the vicar, who gently placed a hand on Bills arm.

Bill looked at the vicar, or rather the place behind the torch where the vicar's voice came from. "Do you know how many kids this monster has abducted and presumably killed? There are windows down the other end of that passage which seem to show views from a pool or something of people weeping – they are wearing animal skins." he snapped his attention back to the goblin. "What are they? Cavemen? How long have you been at this?"

"I understand, and share your sentiments. Our Lord himself said that it would be better for a man to be cast into the sea with a millstone around his neck than to harm a child. I just think it might be unwise to kill our hostage before we have a chance to see if we can use him to get out of here, that's all."

Bill grunted, and a couple of seconds later he released his grip and the goblin fell to the floor gasping.

"Thank you vicar. You're absolutely right." He put his face very close to the goblin's and said "I shouldn't rob the hangman of his job after all. And I will see you swing."

The goblin stopped gasping for breath for a moment to hiss at Bill loudly between it's sharp little teeth which it was bearing.

"Do that again and you won't have any teeth to hiss through!" said Bill.

"We were their Gods!" Spat the goblin.

"What?"

"Your cavemen! We were their Gods, they gave us their children as servants for seven times seven years."

"You were Gods?" asked the vicar, "and what benevolence did you give them? My God died to forgive my sins and rose again to give me eternal life. You were never a God, and when the people found out that you'd tricked them out of their children you just stole them them instead didn't you?"

"It was our right. Humans are so stupid, you are like animals to us. You have never defeated us."

"How's your wing?" Asked Daniel glaring at the prisoners golden eyes shining out of the darkness.

It started to hiss, but Bill was still nose to nose with it and thought better of it.

"What about it's wing?" Asked Bill.

"We had a scrap Sergeant Richmond. He tied me up and dragged me on my back by my arms, and it really hurt. When I got free I walloped him and stamped on his wing. I know it's not what English boys do but I don't care, he had it coming." said Daniel defiantly.

"Well fighting fair is over rated to be honest. I fought in a war with machine guns, shell barrages that lasted for days, poison gas, bayonets and the sharpened edges of spades, not to mention the wire, flame throwers and anything else you can think of. The Huns never fought fair and we didn't fight fair back. Sometimes you can't fight fair or you lose the war, and this piece of filth certainly doesn't. Anyway, we're not in England, are we Daniel? So well done. Do you want to be a Bobby when you're older by any chance?"

"I want to be an engine driver." said Daniel hesitantly,

"Oh well, if you change your mind." smiled the sergeant. He turned to the Goblin, "Never defeat you? You were beaten by an eight year old child who was unarmed and tied up. And I wasn't a lot older when I beat you in a fight either was I?"

The goblin scowled but didn't dare hiss.

Bill ignored it and called to Bob, "What's going on out there Bob? Are there any more of them?"

"Yes Sergeant, not sure how many, but one of them chucked a spear at me so if push comes to shove we've got one extra weapon. Did you bring extra ammo?"

"Yes, one box. It was all that was in the armoury. Fifty rounds. Do you think it will be enough?"

"Let's see shall we?"

He stood up and stood in view of the goblins. There was an excited chatter from the entrance and heads bobbed up and down in an effort to see him clearly.

"This is the police." He said in a commanding tone. "Lay down your weapons and stand clear of the cave."

An arm with a spear came into view. Bob cocked the hammer back on the revolver and raised it to the aim. "Don't be stupid! I am armed and I will.." - the spear was lobbed, The gun roared, once and then once more. The second shot missed, but the first had done it's job and a goblin fell across the entrance, with a hole in it's temple and a confused look on its face. As it hit the floor the gold colour went from it's eyes which turned pale grey and lifeless. The spear followed the pattern of the first one and once it had clattered to a halt, Bob bent down, without taking his eyes, or the gun away from the entrance, picked it up and deposited it with the first one.

Bill stood up from his place by the winged goblin prisoner. "Can you look after this one vicar?"

"It will be my pleasure. If he gives me any trouble I'll set Daniel on him again."

There was a hiss, the thump of a size nine boot and a shriek of pain and indignation. "You were warned." said Bill.

"Perhaps you could throw this one down the well too Daniel." said Emily, "I'll help this time."

The sergeant turned in Daniel's direction. Daniel froze and saw his future life flash before his eyes. He saw handcuffs, saw the judge put the black cap on top of his wig, heard the words "Daniel Smith, for the heinous crime of murdering a goblin by throwing him down a well, I sentence you to death by hanging. You will be taken from here to a place of lawful execution where you shall be hanged by the neck until you are dead. And may God have mercy upon your soul". He almost felt the hangman put the noose around his neck.

"He's a copper!" he hissed at Emily, "Don't tell him that!"

"You threw one of those monsters down a well?" Asked the vicar. "Oh. Well I shouldn't condone violence in my profession, but I think you must have had a good reason?"

"I am going to hang for murder?"

Daniel heard Emily gasp and clasp both hands over her mouth.

"Hang? You should get a medal by my reckoning." Said Bill and laughed. The goblin gasped and blinked it's eyes repeatedly.

"You killed one of my goblins? No!! We are so few!"

"Well, there's even less of you now said Bill. One down and a few more to go."

"No!" screamed the goblin.

"Make that two down." Came Bob's voice, "I've shot one dead."

"No, You liar!" screamed the goblin.

Bob stepped back round the corner, grasped the goblin by the front of its clothing and held it where it could clearly see its fallen brethren.

"Ahhhhhhhhhhhhhhhhhhaaaaaaaaaiiiiiiiiieeeeeeeeeeeeeeee!!" howled the goblin. It buzzed it's wings in an attempt to fly off but Bob had a good grip and slammed it into the cave wall, before pushing it back down round the corner. "Please, don't kill us any more?" bawled the goblin. "We are so few."

Bill stepped around to join Bob and said. I'm putting half the ammunition in your pocket. He undid the bottom right pocket on Bob's tunic and carefully transferred bullets from his own pocket.

Bob remained aiming down the cave. That done, Bill took aim allowing Bob step back into cover in order to open his revolver, remove the three spent cartridges and replace them with live rounds, then he rejoined Bob.

He spoke to Daniel. "Daniel. My rucksack is down by that creature somewhere. Inside is a Thermos flask. Can you pour a cup of tea and offer it round to anyone who wants some please lad? But not that thing, he doesn't get anything!"

"What's a Thermos flask?" asked Emily.

Daniel did as he was bidden, educating Emily in the process. While he was doing that the vicar eased himself down onto the floor next to the goblin. He switched on his torch, the type you put on the front of your bicycle and placed it on its back so that it gave reasonable illumination to the cave.

"How do you do?" he asked politely.

The goblin sniffed at him and seemed appalled at what he smelled. "You are a holy man!" It snarled. "You stink of holiness. Do not touch me!"

"I wasn't planning on it, but we can talk?"

"The chains are burning my wrists. Please take them off. I'm dying!"

"Well, I think taking them off wouldn't be a really smart move would it? But perhaps something between you and the iron might help, hmm?"

With that he pulled out a large handkerchief and a small pen knife from his pockets. He folded the cloth in half and nicked the hem with the blade, and then tore the cloth in two. The goblin watched him with it's golden eyes. Reverend Wetherby wondered how something so evil could have such beautiful looking eyes, then he reflected that even the most evil person had some good in them, although he wasn't sure whether there was any good in anything which lured children into slavery and death. Still, he proceeded with his purpose.

"Turn your back to me, so I can bind this around your wrists."

The goblin obediently wriggled round on its bottom. "Don't touch me holy man." it said

"I'll try not to."

Gently the vicar threaded the cloth through the cuffs and wrapped the steel insulating the goblins wrists. The creature relaxed and sighed.

"Better?" Asked the vicar.

"Yes."

"Now, I have given you something. I want something from you?"

The goblin turned quickly and hissed at him "Holy man!" it spat, "Always you want something for yourself."

"It's not for me. Oh, thank you Daniel." This was because having served tea to the two police officers who were still stood watching the cave entrance. he had poured another cup for the vicar and was now proffering it, it was taking time because there was only one cup on the flask. "Mmm, not bad. Thank you, there's nothing like a brew to pick up your spirits."

The goblin's nose was twitching. "What is that?"

"We call it tea. It's delicious, but it belongs to Sergeant Richmond and he's not going to let you have any I'm afraid."

As he spoke he pulled the hip flask from his pocket and placed the cup on the floor so he could use both hands to open the flask. Once open he wafted the flask upwards beneath his nose inhaling deeply. "Mmmmmm.". He observed that it was having the desired effect, the goblins little green nose was now twitching ten to the dozen, it was comical. The vicar poured a small amount into his tea and swirled it around to mix it. He went to put the flask's cap back on and then feigned to notice the goblin and it's twitching nose. "Oh, would you like to sniff this?" he waved it gently back and forward under it's nostrils which were flaring. It's mouth opened and a little green tongue flickered back and forward over it's lips.

"I'd offer you a drop, but.... you know..."

The goblin looked at the vicar in a pleading fashion.

"Perhaps just a drop then, but don't tell anyone, eh?"

He held the flask to the goblin's lips and tipped it just enough to give a taste.

The goblin gasped and it's face took on a look of sheer wonder. Eyes wide it looked at the vicar, who was shocked by the transformation from fiend to rather cute looking little creature – he wasn't fooled, but effected a bonhomie attitude as one does when one has found a new drinking companion.

"We call that sherry." said the vicar, carefully continuing to wave the flask gently so as to allow it's scent to reach the goblin.

"Now, perhaps we can talk a little?"

"Yes. Can I have more?"

"In a little while. Now, I'm sorry, I didn't catch your name. What's the story with the wings? Why do you have wings but those outside don't?"

"I am a prince, we do not have names, humans have name, we are not humans, Only the royal goblins have wings, our goblins beneath us do not have wings - they do not need them."

"Ah, I see." The vicar gave him another sip of sherry.

"How many of you are there?"

The goblin looked suspiciously at the vicar who shook the flask. The goblin looked at the flask and licked it's lips again.

"I am the last one. Others died, five since I was born, one before. Humans are getting sneaky, they have new weapons and too much iron, when we go to your world they kill us. We have to wait for others to hatch, but we never know when." he looked hungrily at the flask.

Another sip.

"How many goblins are there outside the cave?"

"Eight but HE murdered one!"

"Well, perhaps we may be able to avoid any more killing on either side." said the vicar, "Would you like that?"

"Yes."

Another sip.

And so it continued. A question, an answer, a sip of sherry when the right answer was provided. Within a short while the goblin was in full flow and began chuckling with the vicar as he answered questions.

After a while the vicar got up with help from the children, on account of his wooden leg, and walked over a few yards to the to police officers who were still looking at the entrance where apart from the odd appearance of a goblin head nothing happened.

"You've been having a good chinwag with that thing vicar, have you learned anything useful? Like a secret exit to the cave or something?" said Bob

"Well, maybe a way out. It's difficult to know how far to trust him, even if he is tipsy. Not far I suspect, but it's not like we have too many options and what he is saying seems to make sense."

"Have you been plying my prisoner with alcohol vicar?" asked Bob, shocked.

"Yes, and it seems to have worked, although I fear I will have to get a new hip flask, I don't think I will ever drink from that one again."

"What did it say then?" Asked Bill.

"Well, he doesn't want to lose any more of his troops, so while we've got him as a prisoner I think we can negotiate a safe passage back to the tunnel. The price will be his freedom.

"No! He comes back and stands trial. If we leave him he'll do it again."

"Our objective is to get the kids to safety, once home you can work out a plan of action to stop them coming again. The gateway can be destroyed or made unusable. Perhaps it could be fenced with iron and maintained? And anyway, can you really see a British court trying a little green goblin? This is the twentieth century."

"Well, Emily's cousin placed an iron horseshoe and a rowan cross in the hawthorn patch, we found it when we searched it. That didn't work"

"Well a horseshoe would only work on a limited area. They can be in the proximity of iron as long as they don't touch it."

"Okay, but there are other gateways. We don't know how many or where they are. He'll just pop up somewhere else."

"Well, there are seven gateways. Ordinarily there are seven winged goblins, but they've had a hard time recently and he's the only one left, they are waiting for new ones to hatch, but they don't know when that will happen."

"Hatch? Like eggs?"

"I presume so. The winged ones call themselves royalty, they can only use one gateway – something to do with conflicting magic. I imagine it's a bit like opposing magnets that can't be pushed together."

"Makes sense so far."

"The wingless goblins serve the princes and or princesses maybe if they have them, but anyway, they can't open a gateway, but they can go through any gateway that is opened for them, but they are quite dull brutes who barely have the power of speech and while they might be able to snatch a child, they certainly couldn't coax one into a tunnel, and the only gateway that is openeable at the moment. So they could quite easily be imprisoned here for quite some time."

"He's still getting away with it though. It doesn't sit easy."

"Okay. They feed off the misery. The misery comes from the windows in this cave. In some way watching the parents mourn serves as a tonic for them. I presume there are other caves about but this one is the only one of use to him. If we can destroy the windows then it won't kill him but it will really weaken him. Bob, touch that one of Daniel's house with your pistol. See if it has an effect"

Bob stepped across and did so. At the touch of iron it warped and the picture dimmed, in seconds it was impossible to see an image.

"He's not going to like this." grinned Bob.

"True. We'll have to keep him distracted or blindfold him or something. We need him to work for us." said the vicar.

"How much sherry have you got left?" asked Bill

"About half a flask full, he's only getting sips and he doesn't have much tolerance, but we don't have to get him drunk. Bring him round the corner so he's facing the entrance and we can parley with the enemy while the windows are snuffed out starting at the far end of the cave."

"Sounds like a plan." said Bill. "If we can persuade them to back away we might have a free run to the tunnel."

"I think we can arrange that." said the vicar, "There is one other thing you should know."

"Yes?"

"Time moves differently in here. What feels like a few hours to us is probably a couple of days back home. When we go back through, we will all age according to the time in our world that we've spent in here."

"Ha! I suppose I can put up with a bit of stubble until I can find a razor... oh. Oh no." The policeman physically sagged like a balloon with the air let out of it. "Emily...."

She's already aware of it, "She knows that if she crosses back then it will kill her and that her body will be a pile of bones in seconds. I've, I've err, I've said I will stop with her."

There was a very pregnant pause.

"You will not Reverend. She's my responsibility. It's because of me that she's in here. Now I don't have family, or a flock and I'm a lot older and nearer the end of my life than you are. I'll stop with her. You get Daniel and Bob back."

"You make a good argument sergeant, really you do, but the

decision has already been made. I'm going to work on him a bit more and see if there is any way at all we can get her through, but if there isn't then I will be stopping. Y'know, I've often fancied being a missionary."

"What? Are you serious? Last time I looked in the Bible it said 'great news and glad tidings to all men and peace on Earth. These are NOT men and this is NOT Earth!"

"Hmm, well if I'm going to stay here I do need something to do, and apart from vicaring I don't really know anything apart from tank commanding. And since I don't believe these little beggars have developed tanks yet I find my options somewhat narrowed. Now, I'll go bring our chum around here and have another chat with him and see if I can learn anything else helpful. If you could brief the children on ruining these windows or mirrors or whatever they are, give them one of your torches and any iron you have; keys, handcuffs anything with a bit of iron in it, but the bigger the better and have them start working at the far end of the cave where he can't see what's happening."

In short order the children went walking up the cave, Emily swinging Bills handcuffs and Daniel, despite being warned not to, waving Bob's kukri around like a magic wand, fighting off imaginary enemies, beheading pretend goblins with every slice and clutching the vicar's torch in his free hand. The goblin was brought the opposite way and sat down on the floor. As soon as he appeared there was excitement at the cave entrance and the goblins became a bit more visible.

"Tell them not to try anything, whilst we talk and we'll all come out of this unhurt." said Bill

"Don't try anything whilst we talk and we won't be hurt!" yelled the goblin and grinned at the sergeant.

The vicar sat next to him and smiled. "Drink my friend?" He waved the flask in a friendly fashion.

Daniel and Emily were enjoying themselves alternating in taking turns at destroying the mirrors. Every mirror showed scenes form a different time. The early ones were obviously viewed in the main from water as they had ripples, it seemed that any reflective surface had been used although apart from mirrors on the wall it was difficult to tell what exactly that surface might be. At one point the view appeared to be from the bottom of a leather tankard as it's sides could be seen around the edge whilst above it a man stared into it a man looked down with a sad face and his tears rolled down his rough, reddened face and into the drink making ripples. In the end the children didn't look at the pictures but merely pressed their iron bearing implements to the surfaces until they faded to nothing.

Round the corner, the vicar and his green skinned friend were deep in conversation. The goblin was beginning to slur his words a little. "There may be a way." he said

"Do tell."

"Well, humanses, they die because they're minds can't cope with the knowing of the time that's gone while they weren't there. You. You won't notice because you've been in my kingdom for not long, but Emily, poor Emily; I like her, I really do – she could stop."

"I don't think so, she needs to come home with us. Now you said that there is a way?"

The goblin looked confused and then relieved as it remembered something. "Oh, yes! If they was asleep when they went through then their minds wouldn't mind." it giggled at it's own pun. The vicar didn't bother to laugh now, the goblin didn't seem to notice. "If, if she was asleep then she might live, but she would still be old – nothing would stop that."

"So if we wait for her to fall asleep and carry her through the tunnel she might just be alive when we get to the other side."

"Yesss, but... Sherry?"

"Tell me first, then the sherry."

The goblin made a rasping noise with its lips. The goblins at the entrance perked up and stood in clear view craning to see why their leader was making this odd noise.

"Stay. Back!" Bill commanded them, both he and Bob raised their pistols and the goblins ducked back again.

"But, humans can't sleep here, they are awake for ever, and, and for ever..... Sherry?"

The vicar gave him another sip. And then asked Bill for a hand up. "Step around the corner with me. I think Bob can watch the prisoner and the entrance for a moment.

They could see the kids quite close now extinguishing the mirrors and shining the torch back, presumably to check that nothing was following them in the darkness as children, and many adults, are wont to do.

"So we have to get her to sleep, in a place where insomnia is the norm?" whispered the sergeant.

"Yes." the vicar replied.

"So we're no better off then."

"Well, what about knocking her out cold?"

"Well, it's not that easy. It's not like at the movies where you crack someone over the head and they fall over and wake up five minutes later. She's a child, hit her too hard and she could die from it, don't hit here hard enough and she wakes up too soon and is dead too; it's an option to try but only as a very last resort because the results cannot be guaranteed."

There was a loud snort from round the corner. They stopped talking and Bill stepped back round the corner. After a moment he grinned back at the vicar. "A possible solution presents itself."

The vicar followed him and laughed. "Well it's not ideal and Emily's going to be in for a shock when she wakes up as a sixty

year old woman but it's a better chance than no chance at all."
"How long will the children be? About ten minutes do you think? Let's get ready to go"
"Could someone fill me in please if it's not too much trouble?" Asked Bob.

The children arrived at the last mirror, it was Emily's parents. She stood a while looking at them with tears rolling down her face. "This is the last time I shall see them." she whimpered. Reverend Wetherby took her by the shoulders and turned her to face him. He bent down and embraced her whilst she sobbed into his shoulder.
Bob stepped forward and pressed the cold steel of his pistol into the mirror. In moments it dimmed and extinguished. "It's done." he said.
Bill stepped across to the goblin and tied a length of thin rope he had taken from his rucksack to the middle of the handcuff chain. He ensured that the wings were trapped under the arms, then he nudged the goblin progressively harder with his toe until it stopped snoring and stirred from it's drink induced sleep. "Whaa?"
"Up." said Bob and pulled it to it's feet. "We're going to the tunnel. You are going to tell your goons to back off and give us passage. Once the tunnel is open we will go out and you, much against my better judgement, will be released. Move forwards

when I tell you. If you try to run or trick us I will blow your brains out. Like that one over there." He pointed in the direction of the fallen goblin, who still lay in the entrance. The goblin swallowed hard and looked like it was about to cry. "Are we ready?" Bob asked.

"Nearly." said Bill. "Vicar, could I interest you in a goblin spear?" picking the two spears up off the floor.

"No thank you Bill. I have my trusty walking stick, but perhaps Emily could have one and Daniel too if he gives the kukri back to PC Helen before he slices someone's ear off with it. I do not share my saviour's miraculous ability to restore lost ears when they are removed." he replied, referring to the incident in the Garden of Gethsemane when St Peter chopped off the ear off the priest's servant and Jesus picked it up, rebuked Peter and reattached it moments before he was arrested.

"Good idea vicar."

The swaps were quickly made, the spears, being made for little goblins were well suited to the size of small children.

Finally the vicar pulled out his hip flask and wiped it very thoroughly on a handkerchief. Fortunately vicars are often in the habit of carrying multiple handkerchiefs for the purpose of dealing with people who need to a shoulder to cry on. He handed it to Emily. "Take a big swing and make sure it all goes down for me Emily." he said.

She looked shocked. "It's okay, it's for a good reason, we'll explain later, but you must trust us."

Emily looked uncertain, but took a big gulp and then nearly spat it all out. A big policeman's hand clamped over her mouth just in time. "Drink it down Emily, there's a good girl." said Bill.

She complied and then gasped, "It burns! She said."

"You'll get used to it, but it's important that you drink it."

"Are you trying to get me drunk Billy?"

"Well, we're trying to send you to sleep. That thing over there says if we carry you through asleep then you won't die."

"I haven't been to sleep since I got here, even though I'm weary." she said.

"That's why we're giving you sherry. You'll have some more as we get closer to the tunnel."

"Sherry?" said the Goblin who had heard the magic word

"Move." said Bob to the goblin, prodding it, "and make sure they understand not to get in the way."

The goblin walked forward and nearly fell into the pit. "Stay back and don't hurt us or my friends." it slurred to it's minions, who appeared to understand and obey.

Chapter 24 – The journey home

The little group threaded their way through the trees following the chop marks, as they progressed the trees became easier to identify, they started to take on a wilted and dying look. The goblin was starting to sober up and kept looking at the damaged trees as they passed them, it looked with growing horror at the state of them. "You killed my trees with your iron knife." it spat at long last.
"Be grateful I don't kill you with my iron knife." was Bob's terse reply.

The entire way they were shadowed by the little group of goblins who remained in a single cluster about fifty yards away to the left, well beyond spear range and also beyond accurate pistol range. When they judged that they might be about half way there they stopped and gave Emily another good slug of Sherry. It was a difficult act to get enough alcohol into Emily's system to make sure they could get her to sleep soon after they arrived at the tunnel, but not enough to knock her out before they got there, meaning she would have to be carried, not to mention the possibility of her waking before they got her through to the real world. This time she swallowed it although it brought tears to her eyes, and she spent some time coughing. After a while she giggled. "I think I like that stuff Billy."

Daniel was shocked at her familiarity with Sergeant Richmond, but remembered that she had actually been to school with him. As they walked on Emily remained sober, just more relaxed and chatty if that were possible. Eventually Daniel whispered in her ear. "Ask him about the nettles in the toilet."

She put her hand over her mouth and giggled some more. "Billy?"

"Yes Emily?"

"Was it you that did the things with the nettles to Miss. Ball?"

"What!?"

"You know. Was it you? And did she ever come back?"

"Ermm. Yes, I suppose it was me. What a memory you have! And no she never came back." He glared at Daniel who was sniggering and had the words 'guilty as sin' written across his head.

"I'm glad she didn't come back; you did say she was a witch."

"Something you'd like to confess Bill? It is good for the soul" asked the vicar.

"Be quiet you; you're an Anglican vicar not a Catholic Priest."

Daniel dropped back a little bit to be nearer to Reverend Wetherby and further away from Sergeant Richmond. He looked at the silver knob on the top of the Reverend's walking stick.

"Is that a tank on the top of your stick Reverend?" he asked.

"Yes, my son. It's the badge of the Royal Tank Regiment. I was a 'tankie' in the war before I became a vicar. Tank commanders sometimes need to walk in front of the tank and test to see if it's too boggy for the tank, that's what this is for. Testing to see how deep it is. It's traditionally made of ash."

"Oh, like the one in the park by the hawthorn bush?"

"I don't know Daniel. I haven't noticed but I'll take your word for it."

They stopped again and gave Emily another dose of sherry. There was another giggling fit.

Sergeant Richmond caught Daniel looking at the flask. "Not a chance sunshine. It's medicinal. Have we got enough left vicar?"

"I don't know. I hope so." the vicar replied in a concerned tone.

Suddenly before them they saw the two trees that marked the sides of the tunnel, or at least where the tunnel would be. The trees looked diseased and obviously didn't have long before they collapsed, sap oozed from the wounds Bob had inflicted upon their trunks all the way down to the ground. It looked green and slimy.

"Anyone got the slightest idea how long we've been here?" asked Bob addressing the sergeant and the vicar.

"Not a clue." said Bill.

"Well, I entered the tunnel no more than five minutes after you, but it took a bit longer than that to catch you up. Well, I think it did. You certainly covered more ground than I thought you should have. It really is impossible to tell with time around here."

"Yes." said Bob, "I've noticed my watch is still working but it bears no relation to the time I feel has passed."

Bill looked up from examining his own watch. "Vicar, can you dose Miss Emily up again please. Where the hell do you think you're going?" This was to the goblin who had quietly moved backwards towards one of the damaged trees whilst everyone was looking at their watches and wondering about the passage of time. "I need to rest." hissed the goblin and promptly sat down with his back to the tree."You hurt my shoulder." It lay back, relaxed and closed it's eyes.

"It's just a graze, you won't die from it." said Bill, "Daniel, watch it your spear. You've killed one goblin, if he moves or tries to escape then make it two. No second thoughts don't kill him just skewer him to the tree – we still need him alive." He was watching the pack of goblins who were keeping their distance but were bobbing up and down trying see what was going on.

Emily was choking on the sherry again, but she took it down and smiled at the vicar. "Leading a child to alcohol; I'm going to have to get on my knees and do some penance when we get back young lady." said the vicar.

Emily laughed at him. "Your a nice man." she said slurring her words a little.

"That's just the booze talking."

She giggled again.

"A bit more?"

She nodded and took the flask, this time she drained it and held it upside down to show that it was all gone, and then handed it back to the vicar.

"Sleepy?"

"A little."

Bill took off his cape and laid it on the ground. "Here lie on this and have a kip." he said.

She looked at him, heaved and then turned away and vomited. Daniel started heaving as kids do, and the vicar grabbed him and turned him back toward the goblin "There, now you can't see the sick so you don't need to join in, but if push comes to shove then this is the direction to do it in – he deserves it."

Daniel gulped air and tears pricked his eyes but he kept the contents of his stomach, which admittedly consisted of a cup of tea. The goblin opened it's eyes as slits and then closed them again.

"What do we do now?" said Bill, "She's just brought up all the sherry. We'll never get her to sleep, I think we're going to have to risk KO-ing her."

"Hang on," said Bob. He fetched his rucksack from under his cape, opened it and fished around inside. His hand came out clutching a medicine bottle. He uncorked it and passed it to the vicar who sniffed it suspiciously.

"Gin and tonic?"

"You have a nose for booze Reverend."

"Hmppf!"

"It's for my malaria, I mixed it before we came out, but I haven't felt it since we came in here, so I'd almost forgotten it."

"It's worth a shot. Emily? Try this sweetheart."

"From the bottle reverand? That's so, so …. common.."

Laughs all round. She sat down on Bill's cape and took a swig and screwed her face up."Ewww, I prefer your drink vicar. I think Bob has cheap tastes." She mumbled and smiled her cross eyed smile. She braced herself and took another swig, and then passed out and fell backwards into a prone position.

"Right lets get moving!" said Bill. From his tunic pocket he drew the copper knife, pulled it from it's sheath and pushed it into the impossibly small hawthorn bush which started to transform before their eyes. Bill picked up Emily, still in the sergeants cape, gently in his strong arms and checked her breathing. The vicar looked at her and gently placed his hand on her head.

"Lord, protect this little one, look upon her kindly and see her safe back through to our own world. In your Name we ask this prayer. Amen"

"Amen." said Bob, Daniel and Bill over his shoulder. He turned back to the task in hand, the hole was now a couple of feet wide. They were going to make it.

There was a screech and the goblin, unwatched for a moment seized his chance and leaped at Bill, or rather the knife in Bill's hand. He snatched it with a hand covered in slime from the cut in the tree he had been leaning against. It was this slime that he had quietly worked around his wrists and slid off the handcuffs. Now completely sober and full of fury and hate he went to leap into the air.

Whack! The vicar felled him with a mighty blow to the legs from his stick and Bill dived on him. The goblin screamed and turned, he rammed the knife into Bill's thigh.

Bill roared with pain, but the knife only went in about an inch. The goblin screamed and the knife glowed with a dull orange light and began to smoke, as did the goblin's hand holding the knife and indeed it's arm too. It shrieked and shrieked, before their eyes the arm crisped and blackened steadily from the hand towards the elbow, then there was a slight flash and the knife was gone. Bill reeled backwards into the hollow which had formed in the hawthorn bush. He was reaching into his tunic and drew his pistol which he aimed at the fleeing goblin who was running and hopping towards it's little band.

"No! Don't wake the girl!" said Bob who was still holding Emily.

"It's too late! The knife vanished. He managed to stab my old war wound, I felt the blade grate against the shrapnel which is still in there!"

"Steel shrapnel?" asked the vicar.

"I have a knife, he dropped it when we were scrapping." Said Daniel breathlessly feeling in his pockets. He did this several times. "Oh no!" he searched again. "It must've dropped out when

I let Emily dry her face on my jacket by the pool." he wailed.

"Kill them!" shrieked the goblin who had reached the safety of his friends.

Bill aimed his pistol.

"Sergeant! Look at the hawthorn!" yelled Bob.

The hole where Bill was leaning was still growing, within moments the tunnel was complete."

"I think it fused with the shrapnel – it's still working!" Said Bill

"Well don't just stand there man move! Make sure it's open all the way. " yelled the vicar. "Daniel get in there, Bill, you and Emily get in there, I'll bring up the rear."

A spear was thrown and landed well short. The horde of seven goblins, minus their brave leader were bounding towards them whooping and screaming, slashing with their swords. The vicar backed into the tunnel bumping Bob along. "Keep going Bob, keep going, don't stop!"

Suddenly they were round the corner. Bill stumbled out and fell onto the soft English grass. Daniel tripped over him and Bill yelled as he caught the knife wound. Bob dropped Emily in Bill's lap and spun around. The vicar was still backing out. A goblin stuck it's head around the corner and ran at him. The vicar slammed the silver knob of his stick into its eye and was rewarded by a squawk. He tumbled out backwards. The Goblin put a hand to it's injured eye and rushed forward, there was now another one behind it. There was a click of a pistol hammer being cocked and the goblin stopped within an inch of the muzzle of Bob's revolver. Bob smiled, the Goblin gaped and Bob flicked the weapon sideways into the hawthorn. There was a collective scream from the goblins and the hawthorns snapped shut closing the tunnel in an instant and grazing Bills outstretched hand in the process.

It was dark in the park. They all dropped in a loose group on the sweet smelling grass. "How's Emily?" Bob asked.
"Not good. She's breathing, but it's fast and shallow." said Bill who was cradling her in his arms.
Bob shoved the revolver back into his tunic, drew his whistle and blew hard, long and repeatedly. It was answered within seconds, by one, and then another whistle. Very shortly running feet could be heard.
"We're in the park." Yelled Bob. "Get an ambulance!"

Chapter 25 – Loose ends

It turned out they had been gone three days, all the men's faces itched like crazy for a while as the stubble caught up.

Emily was rushed to hospital and was in a critical state for several days, but she recovered. She aged forty nine years in a matter of a week. The doctors were perplexed, they had admitted a child and found themselves treating a lady in her late fifties. Emily knew her name but appeared to have lost a lot of memory and spoke a lot of nonsense about goblins and strange lands. If she hadn't been so ill she would have been committed to a lunatic asylum. Eventually she was accepted as the girl who had disappeared almost fifty years before, it was splashed all over the papers for several days, but since Emily couldn't tell them anything interest faded quickly.

The police officers knew better than to come out with a fairy story and feigned amnesia. It didn't sit well their superiors but since they had retrieved not one but two missing children there wasn't a lot that could be done. The ammunition was replaced and placed back in the armoury with the pistols before their absence could be noticed.

When they got the chance Bill and Bob returned to the park, in the dead of night, where they were met by the vicar with a coil of barbed wire and some steel pegs to hold it in place. After several hours of toil and being scratched and stabbed by barbed wire they had succeeded in weaving the wire in and out of the hawthorn bush and were satisfied that the iron in the wire would keep the goblins in their place for some time to come. It wouldn't have taken half so long if the 'magic shrapnel' as Bob put it, in Bill's leg hadn't kept trying to open the tunnel.

When they had finished Bill announced to Bob that he would be retiring from the police force. "Emily will need someone to look after her." he said.

"You?" asked Bob. "Won't her cousin be doing that? You know, the one who put the horseshoe in there?"

"She's not really capable, she always was a bit funny. I made enquiries and it seems she too busy collecting stray cats for looking after anyone else. Besides which it seems she's not that sure that it is Emily."

He was as good as his word. Bill worked his last shift the day before Emily was released from hospital. She was still very frail but thanks to Bill's constant attention she steadily became stronger. Bill temporarily turned his front room into a bedroom for her as she was too weak for stairs, which caused tongues to wag. Two years after returning from the goblin's land, she was fully recovered and it was the vicar's privilege to marry them both at St Bart's. Bill had dug out his police uniform and against regulations he wore it one last time, Bob was his best man and wore his uniform too replete with the brand new silver chevrons of a sergeant. Bill and Emily lived happily into old age together and eventually her lost years seemed like a distant bad dream to Emily.

One night Bill awoke to find a visitor in his room. It was the angel he had seen at Mons. He didn't feel frightened by the angel this time. They stood by the bed talking quietly.
"I told you that your prayers would be answered and that one day you would understand why you were wounded. Do you understand now?" The angel asked him.
"Yes, we wouldn't have got home if the shrapnel hadn't been there to absorb the knife. Thank you for being there for me. It was a shame the war wasn't over by Christmas though. All those poor lads who never saw hearth and home again. And yes, my prayers were answered – she came back – Thank you." He turned to see if Emily had been disturbed and noticed for the first time his own form lying still in bed beside her.
"Ohh.." he paused, "Will she be alright?"
The angel nodded and smiled. "She will be looked after and well guarded."

Shortly after Bill died Emily moved into a care home where she lived to a ripe old age and made the staff smile with talk of being visited at night by fairies. One night, Jasmine, a plump Jamaican carer with a huge heart and an equally huge smile saw a faint golden glow coming from under Emily's door, putting her ear to the door she heard the sounds of Emily laughing and faint sounds like the whirring of birds wings. She peered through the lock and saw Emily sitting up in bed. Little lights bobbed around her and some of them rested on her bed, they appeared to have a human form. Suddenly one of the lights flew straight towards the keyhole and the hole was filled with a tiny face framed with delicate wings. Two tiny glittering eyes were staring straight into her eye. Jasmine fell backwards onto her ample bottom. She heard laughter like the tinkling of little bells and then scrabbled madly back to her feet and ran squealing to the staff room where she barricaded the door. Once she'd done that she blocked the keyhole with tissue paper and sellotape. Then for good measure she did the same to the crack under the door. She spent the rest of her shift sitting in the furthest corner of the room from the door clutching the tiny gold cross on the necklace around her neck before her. She refused to work nights after that.

A few nights later her replacement on the night shift reported seeing a young looking policeman walk past the staffroom door. It struck her that the uniform was not the current nineteen seventies style. His police number was not on his epaulettes but on his collar which was the stand up type rather than the more modern open type with a shirt and tie. He was holding hands with an equally young lady in an equally old fashioned wedding dress with long locks and a noticeable squint. They were smiling at each other and laughing although strangely she heard no sound. She followed them but lost them as they turned a corner by the entrance. The door was locked and bolted from the inside. Not believing in ghosts she put it down to a waking dream and went back to the staff room. The next morning it was discovered that Emily had passed away peacefully in her sleep. In her hand was a photograph frame which showed her and Bill on their wedding day.

Daniel tried to tell the true story but not surprisingly was not believed. Angela and his mom put it down to the stress of being kidnapped by persons unknown, much as she blamed stress when a few hours after returning home, for no good reason that she could discern, he smashed the mirror in the back room to smithereens with her flat iron. She was just glad to have her little boy back. Even Angela forgave him for the worm in her shoe.

On a visit to London a few years later he fell in love with the Underground. Apparently he was still attracted by tunnels and caves. As a young man he moved to London and fulfilled his childhood dream of being a train driver - on the tube trains.

Since he retired he has written books on both the Underground and the supernatural, sometimes combining the two. He still uses the Underground on a daily basis. People sometimes notice that he doesn't have many mirrors in his house.

Bob along with the vicar, until the latter's retirement under Church of England rules meant he had to move away from his parish, kept a watch on the hawthorn bush in the park.

Bob was a regular visitor to Daniel's house, popping down from Beare-in-the-Green, After he died his kukri passed to Daniel to whom he had willed it. Daniel hung it above his bed – which went down about as well with his wife as did his hatred of mirrors.

Epilogue – The present day

Jessica stood chatting and smoking with her friend Rachel. Both young women had their toddlers on reins and the children gurgled to one another happily. Their mothers were looking at the large pile of rusty barbed wire which the council workmen had ripped out of the bushes behind them. It was still entwined with hawthorn branches and accumulated litter and was surrounded by orange mesh plastic barriers. It was awaiting collection and disposal by another council environmental team, otherwise known as the refuse collectors, later in the week. They were discussing the fact that Evangeline Steptoe's little boy Franklin had managed to get into the bush and gashed his hand on the rusty wire requiring stitches and a tetanus injection. Evangeline had been in touch with a claim company before she left the accident and emergency department of the hospital and was looking now for compensation, hence the council rooting it out. No one could work out why the wire had been placed in the hawthorn bush – it was obviously a stupid thing to have done.

A few yards behind them Charmaine, Jessica's other child, a three year old daughter by her ex-boyfriend, was looking quietly and shyly at the funny little green man with wings who had emerged from a tunnel in the bush. He had a little knife on his belt, and one of his arms looked strange; black and withered by his side, but he had a nice smile and beautiful golden eyes which twinkled, she looked back at her mom who was still talking and not paying her any attention, and then once again back at the little green man. He grinned at her and beckoned with his good hand.

"Fairy!" she said pointing at him, as giggling and laughing she trotted towards him.

The End

Printed in Great Britain
by Amazon